SLAUGHTER ON GIGGLETIME MOUNTAIN

SHINGLES: BOOK 10

DREW HAYES

AUTHORS & DRAGONS

Tabitha screamed as she swung, the pain, fury, and loss of her last few hours all poured into the final strike. As the crackling axe struck, it carved through the bunny-masked man's sternum, cleaving down into the man's chest as he lay rising from the ground. The blow sank entirely through his torso, into the wood of the floor below, pinning his heart in place. For a moment, the killer twitched and spasmed, before finally, mercifully, growing still.

The flying sparks from the axe grew fewer and fewer, until Tabitha was left with only the fading glow of her weak flashlight. She stood there, waiting, making sure that Mr. Giggles didn't so much as move a finger. There had been too many fake-outs already. This time, she had to make sure he stayed dead.

To her shock, as she shone the light across the body, most of the corpse had already turned to dust. Only the heart showed no signs of deterioration, though it was warped and misshapen, just as legends said. Footsteps came from the stairs behind her, causing Tabitha to swing her flashlight around, nearly blinding an old man descending the walk, holding a bloody gash on his shoulder.

"Repairman Dougal! You're alive?"

"Seems I'm not free of those alimony payments just yet. Managed to duck one of the broken sawblades and save my head, but I had to patch the shoulder before I could move. Old bones can't handle much blood loss." The handyman walked over to Tabitha's side, looking down at the pile of dust, the skull, and the axe. "Was worried I'd be too late, but clearly that's not an issue."

She nodded, staring at the dust as through she didn't trust it not to swirl back to life. "I hate the idea of violence; I just couldn't let him hurt more people. Killing him was the only way."

"Take heart, lass. Whatever man this once was, he's been dead for a long time. After tonight, I'll seal this room off and purge it from the maps and records," Dougal assured her. "If we're smart and dedicated, maybe your group can be the last one. The nightmare can end, and at long last, this poor soul can finally know peace."

Blood pooled at the base of the chair as Ghoul finished carving up the final victim. Her face was covered by a mask of withered flesh that would have been horrifying, if not for the scene around it making it mere plastic by comparison. Five bodies, all in various states of dismantlement, were spread throughout the cabin. The bald one who'd tried to scare them off with a shotgun was last, Ghoul's razors and knives going back into the bag at her side as she left his corpse in the chair. Usually, Jester took the last kill, but sometimes when prey was especially troublesome, he turned them over to Ghoul at the end. It wasn't that she had a sterner stomach, simply that she was more adept at keeping someone alive for as long as she wanted. The others got excited, or impatient. Ghoul didn't let the game end until she was ready; the reaper could god damn well wait his turn.

Burlap lumbered in from around a corner. He moved with unnerving quiet for a man that size. It seemed like magic, but it was really just the practice of being a big man moving carefully through a small world. Personally, Ghoul also thought it helped that Burlap never talked, not even when he lacked the head-covering sack with a pair of eyeholes. The man lived in silence, both during these times and in the real world, so by Ghoul's thinking it made sense that silence would have his back.

"No lights, no cops in waiting, looks like this one went clean once again." The voice came from behind Burlap, as another man stepped out. His mask was not terrifying or well-crafted; it looked like it had come from the discount bin of a Halloween store. Which, in fact, it had. The rubbery werewolf mask was short more than a few hairs and had lost its paint in several spots; however, it did successfully conceal the owner's face, which was the core requirement of these jobs.

"Hitting these cabins was a stroke of genius," Wolf continued. "Way easier than trying this in places with neighbors. No close calls anymore."

A single step echoed from the hall, and every eye turned in that direction. From the shadows emerged a man in a ceramic mask. The covering had a huge red smile, bruise-purple cheeks, and flashes of green around the eyes. Aside from that, he looked downright fashionable, clad in a crisp gray suit. The ensemble was high-end and custom-made, just like the mask, one more sign of the dedication Jester brought to his craft. He had been the first of them, and deep down, they knew when their end came, he would be the last.

"No close calls," Jester agreed. "And yet, no challenge either. Our practice has betrayed us; our own skills have stolen the joy of the hunt."

The others waited, silent. When Jester talked like this, something new was brewing. Something dangerous, and exciting. "I think, perhaps, it is time we found a fresh horizon, pushed ourselves past the limits of comfort once again. To be alive is to grow, without new challenges we're not better than the corpses we leave behind. If you are interested,

I have a new lead. Something quite different, and yet in a way, truly classic. Will you follow?"

Ghoul was first, by virtue of being the smartest of the three remaining. Well, the smartest that talked, it was hard to know how much Burlap had going on upstairs. She lowered her head, whispering the words she knew by heart. "Always."

Wolf was only a few seconds behind; he was an excellent follower, if nothing else. "Always."

Since Burlap didn't speak, his subservience was shown, rather than told. The huge man simply lowered himself to both knees, and then bowed before Jester.

The pledges drew a nod from Jester, who walked over to the chair where the final body was still cooling. "Then sharpen your implements, my beloved disciples. We have a very… entertaining destination for our next outing."

1

ori popped open the door of her run-down sedan and winced as she accidentally looked up into the afternoon sun. It hurt, but the relief of stretching her legs was more than enough to compensate for the minor eyeball searing. From the other side of the car, Horace and Bernard piled out, already reaching back for the equipment. They were consummate professionals in how they treated the equipment, even while bickering constantly about what should go where and how to handle what.

"Coriander Smith?" She winced at the sound of her full name, even as she waved to the young man with a clipboard who'd just called it. All things considered, Cori could understand why her mother, growing up with a name like Jane Smith, would decide to give her daughter something more interesting. Cori only wished the woman had perhaps put a bit more thought into the decision.

"Just Cori is fine, thanks."

"I'll make a note," the clipboard wielder said, not actually bothering to make any markings on whatever paper the mysterious board concealed. "You're here for the web-based promotional outreach team, correct?"

"Maybe? I met with a bunch of people in suits; they all sort of looked the same to me." Cori shrugged, as if to say she didn't feel particularly bad about that admission. "Our channel does documentaries on restoration of classic sites, houses, natural wonders, all that stuff. The impression I got is that they wanted a live version of that. Shoot video of changing out the rides, re-purposing the buildings, that sort of thing."

This time, the man did produce a pen and make a few scribblings, although what they were remained concealed. "That's the long-term plan, sure, but for this weekend we're just looking to get key shots of our people carefully assessing the property and thinking deeply on how to make it great." He paused, looking over the sheet quickly. "But you do have full access to the property, excluding places blocked for safety concerns. Looks like they want you taping a lot of 'before' footage between the important shots. Come on, I'll take you to your quarters."

"Thanks, Mr…" Cori let the words trail off, making sure to draw attention to the fact that he'd yet to so much as give a name.

"Just Ajax is fine. The titles belong to people with power. I'm only an intern."

Two figures strode into view from behind the car, both laden down with equipment. The slightly taller of the two, stuck out a hand to shake. "Pleasure to meet you Ajax. I'm Horace Miller." Ajax accepted the hand, giving it a well-practiced shake, before looking to the other one.

"Huh? Oh, I'm Bernard Miller. Nice to meet you." Bernard took Ajax's already offered hand and gave it a quick pump before turning his attention back to the bags.

Cori made sure to enjoy the confusion that came next as

Ajax looked at both men, then at his clipboard, before glancing toward her, clearly looking for help. She was tempted to let him twist, but they were on this shoot for a few days. Ajax or someone like him would probably be their handler, so laying a little diplomatic groundwork at the outset might make the whole process easier. Besides, she had a hunch he was used to taking shit from his bosses, so getting off easy would be a welcome reprieve.

"No, they aren't related, it's just a coincidence." It came up every time, and not without some cause. On top of sharing the same name, Horace and Bernard had gone to the same college, with the same major, and been in most of the same classes. Hell, they even bickered like siblings. That said, the two men *looked* substantially different. Bernard was stout and solid, with a wild beard that may or may not have been leaning into the fantasy-dwarf style his body defaulted to. Horace, on the other hand, was tall and muscular with a completely shaven head, from the neck to the scalp. For some reason the combination of matching name and dissimilar appearance made everyone who wanted to ask the obvious question of relation visibly uncomfortable.

"I see." Ajax made another note, but he did look relieved to have the matter done with. "Please take everything you need from the car. We'll have to take a shuttle over the old bridge to get into the park, so trips back will be limited. Cori, when you and your team are ready, meet me over at the white van."

Not the warmest of invites, however he did use her preferred name, which Cori chose to take as a positive sign. That was largely by necessity, on projects like this being an optimist was a survival strategy. When one started to think things were going wrong, they made bad choices. Cori preferred to keep a positive outlook and a cool head on her whenever possible. Besides, they were just shooting footage of corporate raiders drooling over their new prize: a formerly abandoned amusement park. Compared to the locations they'd had to sneak onto, many of which were structurally unsafe, to say nothing of the wildlife that had moved in, this was going to be easy money.

Were Cori a little more practical and less positive, she might have recognized that thought as chumming the waters of fate. Instead, she and the others boarded the van, ready to get their first sight of Giggletime Mountain.

2

"In its prime, Giggletime Mountain was one of the best draws in all of the state. The park theming was originally built around Mr. Giggles, a beloved cartoon rabbit from those old-timey shorts we all know and love. Fun fact: Mr. Giggles' likeness would later be bought and repackaged as Floppy Smokes, the pro-cigarette bunny."

Looking out the window, Cori could see the cracked and overgrown roads all leading to the same bridge where they were headed. She knew everything the driver was telling them; that was part of her prep for a shoot. Well, except for the smoking rabbit part—she had to admit this driver had some deep trivia knowledge. Her mind was half-listening to the facts, mostly focused on all the things they had to do, and how they should start. Kicking things off well laid the groundwork for success, and she wanted to be sure they did well on this. Internet videos didn't pay the way they used to; this was a stepping stone into working with corporate partners, getting her team some real sponsorship. When she was younger, she'd have called this selling out, but it was a far smaller compromise than giving up on her dream and taking a normal job like her parents wanted. Too bad for them, don't name a child after a spice if you don't want them to stand out.

"That's fascinating! If you don't mind though, what I'd really love to know more about are the murders." Horace was leaned forward, eyes gleaming as he took in every detail that the driver spoke. Next to him, Bernard snorted. "She's not going to tell us that. Nobody wants to talk about those."

"No, it's okay; I don't mind giving you folks a proper warning." The driver checked her mirrors as she pulled onto the bridge. It ran from the mainland over to Giggletime Mountain, which was admittedly well-named. Surrounded by the river on all sides, it was a spear into the skyline, a natural wonder that had been quickly co-opted for commerce. The river's churning waters below drew Cori's eye. They were beautiful, and deadly if one were to fall in. She loved that combination, and regretted that her cameras were all packed. It might have made for a nice opening shot.

Once they were past the first of the bridge, where the rough terrain rattled the van and made talking impossible, the driver continued. "There're a lot of stories that go around about this place. They say enough people died on this land to fill the river with blood. Not true, by the way. Still, there is no denying that people were killed here, the tales get that right. That, and the lightning. It all started with the lightning."

Despite herself, Cori felt a slight chill at the words. This woman must have told the story countless times; she'd gotten good at putting the right touches on it.

"It started as a simple accident. Storm was blowing in, and it caught the wrong end of a tent, sent it flying. The canvas eventually got tangled up in a coaster's wheels, bringing the car to a stop on the track, at the mercy of the arriving storm. This was the sixties, you understand, before we had all the tech and safety features. The man working as Mr. Giggles heroically leapt into action without even taking time to remove his costume head, grabbing a fire axe and climbing onto the tracks to cut them free. He succeeded, you know. People don't talk about that enough, but he did get them free. Unfortunately, no good deed goes unpunished, and the man got hit by three lightning strikes simultaneously. No one had ever seen anything like it, but it's also not often we have someone stand on a coaster holding a metal tool in the middle of a storm."

"And then he killed a bunch of people?" Bernard asked, finally showing more interest in their subject matter.

The driver eyed Bernard coolly through her mirror. "Some say the lightning addled his brain, leaving nothing but the urge to kill. Others believe it wasn't a natural storm at all that blew in that day. Giggletime Mountain's biggest competition was a haunted park, rumored to be run by a true practitioner of the dark arts. It was an evil, cursed storm that came to the shores, and that dark magic corrupted the poor man. Whatever you believe, yes, when Mr. Giggles rose from the ground, his oversized pink rabbit head still burned and smoking, people thought it was a miracle. Then he began to swing that horrible axe, and the night filled with screaming."

Cori decided to speed things along. "Eventually brought to a close when police arrived. They say it took a dozen gunshots to slow him down. One of the officers even cut him with his own axe a few times once he was on the ground; Mr. Giggles refused to stay put. They finally subdued him, by which I mean killed him, and the remains were buried. That was that, until the first copycat arrived."

Something flickered in the driver's gaze, a dark sentiment

that didn't manage to reach her words. "Many believe the story of Giggletime Mountain is one of murderous copycats making a pilgrimage here to kill in Mr. Giggles' name. Others think it is one killer, the same killer, cursed to rise, murder, and die, over and over in an endless cycle. Regardless, eventually the bad press took its toll. Giggletime Mountain couldn't compete with other parks that had big name characters and no reputation for guests getting butchered. Population shifted, this area became out of the way, and the gates shut for good."

"Until Gentrification Investments found out about an opportunity just waiting to be claimed," Ajax said. It was the first time he'd piped up since they got in the van; he'd been completely absorbed in his clipboard thus far. Cori was surprised he'd even been listening. "The remote location and existing structures make it perfect. The company will pull away all the sillier theme park elements, build luxury housing, install some docks, add cell towers for proper service, and eventually build this useless husk into a private resort for the wealthy. Exclusivity is the new popularity, and this place will only be for those who truly belong."

Horace leaned forward, sticking his head into the front seat section so he could fix Ajax with a stare. "You don't really get the concept of amusement parks, do you? They're supposed to be fun for everyone."

"That's why they all charge so much at the gates?" Ajax countered. "Pay to play has always been part of the model; my bosses are just taking it to the next natural evolution."

Cori ignored the arguing; now that the conversation had turned from history she'd lost even a passing interest. There was work to focus on, and she intended to do it well. The story of Giggletime Mountain was one that deserved to be told. She would give them the nice, pro-restoration footage the company wanted, but she'd also shoot enough to tell the truth about Giggletime Mountain, once her finances were secure and her platform was bigger. Her only worry was that there wouldn't be enough interesting footage to make something out of.

By the next dawn, she would truly realize how ridiculous of a fear that had been.

3

The four people sitting in an unremarkable minivan were not wearing masks. Strangely, this made several of them feel less like themselves. Over time, those identities had grown larger in their lives, taking over more and more of who they'd been. Nowadays, they only used their actual names around other people. With or without the masks, they knew who they were.

"An isolated park, surrounded by water on three sides and a steep drop on the fourth. Cell service out here is spotty, by the time we're on the other side of the bridge, expect it to fail entirely. We'll still rig up some jammers though, just to be safe. When dealing with people who have this kind of money, there's no telling what sort of resources they can tap if they get word out."

"We're killing rich ones this time?" Wolf was poking his head through the narrow space between the front seats, some of his brown patchy beard being tugged on by the cheap material. This was just one of the many reasons they torched their vehicles after use, too many casual DNA samples could be left behind.

Jester glared down for several seconds before finally deciding to answer. His face, like his mask, was largely featureless unless he was purposely wearing an emotion. "I didn't plan it that way, but when prey puts itself in such a perfect trap, there's no reason not to spring it. The people attending this assessment are corporate raiders, people who buy up existing businesses to gut or take over them, so naturally they have access to a lot of capital. There are also some insurance assessors who are deciding what the minimum amount of safety repairs they can make are before it gets cheaper to pay out injury claims, and a few local politicians to make sure the project doesn't hit any red tape. The whole event is being couched as a celebration and evaluation, which I assume means lots of rich people indulging in their favorite sins away from the prying eyes of the public."

"It's almost like someone stocked this whole place specifically with the kinds of people who could be casually slaughtered without making an onlooker feel ethically conflicted."

"Wolf, stop looking into the camera while you talk," Jester snapped. While he'd been giving the explanation, Wolf had taken out one of the night-vision cameras and begun fiddling with the lens.

He jerked his head back up, catching Jester's eyes. "Sorry, when I'm bored I do equipment checks. Point stands, though."

As far as bad habits, admonishing Wolf for checking their supplies was probably counter-productive. There were far worse ways the man could use his nervous energy. Rather than verbally smacking him on the nose yet again, Jester merely continued detailing the plan. "Once we've cut all landlines and jammed the cells, we take out the bridge. Given its overall disrepair, I'm sure Burlap can make it look like an accident. And even if he doesn't, by that point they'll be trapped. Hunting unaware prey is fun, but eventually they'll catch on regardless."

From the backseat next to Wolf, Burlap gave a silent nod. Heavy lifting and mechanical work, including demolitions, were what gave him a role on the team. If Jester wanted the bridge gone, it would be gone as soon as he gave the order.

"Should we ready disguises?" Ghoul had been sitting patiently, listening to the plan unfold, carefully considering each piece as Jester laid it forth. He never told them the plans until it was almost time to act, just one more reminder that he was the heart of this operation while they were merely his tools. "To blend in with so many suits, I presume we'll need some ourselves."

Jester's smooth face wrinkled suddenly as he smiled at Ghoul, a clear reward for her perception. "Close, very close, but not quite. These are the kind of people who would look someone else wearing a suit in the eyes, and we don't want to leave memories. I've procured us some simple sanitation jumpsuits. There's a day crew doing clean-up, although they'll be gone before the night falls. It should provide enough cover to do all the prep work we need, and none of the prey will pay attention to the help unless they're about to trip over them."

From his pocket, Jester produced a folded stack of pages. Laying them flat against the dash, he revealed photocopies of very dated blueprints. "Once the sanitation staff is kicked out, there will still be an hour or so before we can begin our work. I dug through the park's plans, and they have several old areas that were sealed off. Some for safety reasons, some pragmatically, and a few without explanation. I've found one centrally located to hide in while we wait to begin, but you'll each need to memorize them all. When panic sets in, these are what will allow us to escape detection until we're ready to strike again."

"How long do you think we can keep it up for?" Wolf asked.

"Ideally? Until the last one is gone. Imagine what a spectacle it would be, an entire group mysteriously wiped out, and with a convenient local legend to soak up the blame. However, if complications arise, I've prepared an escape method for us. That's all you need to know for now."

Turning the van on, Jester drove not toward the bridge, but over behind a cluster of trees where they'd be able to change. As he drove, Jester's face shifted as well. Wrinkles appeared, laugh lines, an expression of weary boredom like he'd seen on so many people with mundane jobs. This was no magical force or supernatural gift, just the practice of a man who'd had to learn facial control through intent rather than instinct. By the time they arrived, he'd look like any other day-worker, ready to get the job done so he could move on with his life.

That was why Jester could never give the lifestyle up. He was one of the only people he'd ever met who truly loved his work, and that was too rare to let go of. Today was looking especially bright, and Jester could scarcely wait for the sun to fall. Once it did, the real job started.

4

The park was bad. Not completely derelict, although it very well might have been before Cori's arrival. Seeing teams of sanitation workers scuttling around betrayed the fact that they'd probably been doing some work already. While she did like authenticity in her videos, places left alone for this long could probably use a good sweep before going on camera. Stumbling across a nest of animal corpses, or worse, living wild animals, slowed everything down. Trash was fine; only the truly gruesome stuff would have to be edited out. Even aside from demonetization concerns, Cori tried to keep her content generally accessible, casting as wide a net as possible.

In truth, bad was good for what she needed. Without a shitty, rundown park to film at the top, the new, sparkling finished version wouldn't look as good in contrast. If the final park was a five out of ten, it would shine all the brighter when compared to where it started, which ranked somewhere around a negative three. The trash, the frayed tents, the stained signs, the weather damage, all of it came together to paint a picture of neglect and waste.

None of the rides were working, of course. They had people out looking them over, although not too many. Cori couldn't help noticing that most of the executives who'd been arriving immediately went right to the housing building, dropping off their bags and hunkering down in closed-door meetings that she wasn't permitted near.

She had been a little surprised by the on-site housing, but, considering the geography, it made sense. Even before the world stopped caring, getting here must have been something of a drive. A hotel allowed guests to stay longer and spend more, while also offering a spot to let employees live. Keeping them on property meant they were always available to work, and cut down on fears about people missing shifts. Cori and her team had been set up in old employee quarters, which came with four walls, half-rotted desks, and dusty beds. The people in suits were using the hotel rooms, which Cori took a small comfort in knowing their accommodations couldn't be *that* much better. Father Time didn't play favorites; everything here was old, no matter how nice it had once been.

They used the afternoon to get as many daylight shots of Giggletime Mountain as possible. It was a large park, especially considering the age. Rides dotted the landscape, retreating only from the midway and food courts, where large gathering spaces had once been needed. There were also empty stores and service stands; all branded with the Giggletime Mountain characters. Mr. Giggles was on nearly all of them, of course, his giant pink ears poking up even in crowded shots. Frequently, he was joined by Admiral Raccoon, Dr. Puddin, and Albatross Esquire, who were apparently more common in the Giggletime mythos than less popular ones, like Squirts the Pooping Turtle.

"Why is the raccoon an admiral?" Bernard asked as they wandered under an old sign advertising ice cream, with the special bonus that the staff was now washing their hands as they served customers. "I mean, they've got an albatross right there, and those are sea birds. Makes more sense to have him be the admiral and make the raccoon the lawyer."

"I'm impressed you know what esquire means," Horace said. "And the answer is obvious. It's a cartoon. They mixed up the roles because it makes less sense, and is therefore funnier. There's nothing unexpected about finding an albatross around a boat, seeing him wearing a tiny suit with a briefcase in his beak, that's more entertaining."

Cori turned, catching a few sanitation workers who were cleaning up near the Ferris wheel entrance. One of them, a thick man with a patchy beard, looked up, catching sight of her filming. His eyes went wide, so Cori gave a big smile and a cheerful wave, making sure he knew it was fine. They'd just cut around the part where he actually looked into the lens, no big deal. He kept staring at her for a few seconds, finally managing a shameful expression as he turned away. Poor guy must think he'd really messed up the shot.

"At least it makes more sense than the doctor. That one is just a lump of brown with a stethoscope and googly eyes. Looks more like Dr. Turd than Dr. Puddin." Bernard grumbled even as he swapped out batteries on his camera, throwing the spent one onto a portable charger equipped to his belt. Bernard often looked, and acted, like an overburdened pack mule, but he had a system for dealing with the equipment that no one else was allowed to be part of. It worked, so Cori let it be. As long as he could do the job well, there was no reason to complain about how he did it.

"Mr. Giggles is still the worst," Horace replied. "Something about his eyes. Too wide. Too excited. Even without all the murder legends, that rabbit gives me the creeps."

"Good point." Cori swung away from the sanitation workers, up to the ice cream sign. "Let's get plenty of Mr.

Giggles footage. Since we won't have a real killer to film, we can use sign shots whenever we talk about the urban legend. Add a little music and lighting in post, we can make it feel unnerving, get the viewer into the right frame of mind."

Behind her, the bearded sanitation worker looked up once more, carefully committing Cori, and her friends, to his memory. He'd have to take care of them sometime tonight, ideally before Jester found out. If Wolf came back and told their leader what happened without the tape in hand, there would be no discussion or debate. He'd just kill Wolf where he stood, and the others would step lightly over his corpse. That was the cost of working with other murderers.

5

Ghoul was the last to arrive. This was not due to poor planning or inefficient use of time; she was late because her job had involved the most legwork. Everyone had their own tasks, and as the best infiltration artist of the group, she was selected for the stealthiest errands. Burlap had been rigging the bridge, Wolf was making a layout of the park, Jester did whatever Jester deemed needed doing, and Ghoul was in charge of disabling outward communication.

With cellular service already spotty, most people probably wouldn't even realize that signal jammers had been set up through the park, piggybacked onto the few working electrical systems still running. Cutting the landline was a tad more obvious, which was why she'd waited as late in the day as possible to do it. Once the bridge went down, it wouldn't matter, but anything that could tip off their prey before the trap was sprung risked the entire enterprise. Some risk was inevitable, however, which was why Jester instructed her to simply make the move near evening.

The sun dipped low overhead, almost kissing the horizon, as she arrived at the meeting spot. They'd need to rest for the next few hours, recovering their strength from a day of prep, while the prey tired themselves out. Midnight was usually the best time to get things started; all the responsible people were asleep, and the irresponsible people were compromised. If history held true, they'd be looking at an entire park of easy targets by the time they were ready to move.

Finding the door wasn't easy. This location was tucked away near an old cluster of maintenance worker buildings. Inside one was what appeared to be the remains of a false wall that had been scraped away, as well as a *very* serious lock lying on the ground. Ghoul paused to admire the hunk of metal, turning it over in her hand. Heavy, reinforced, this must have been top of the line when it was made. Of course locks, and lock-picking technology, had grown tremendously over the years. Had Ghoul been present for this obstacle, she felt confident she'd have been able to get them through with a hairpin and a few minutes to work.

Instead, they'd used a method more suited to Burlap. The lock was still cold from where it had been sprayed with liquid nitrogen, and shards of it were on the ground near where it must have been struck from the door. Freeze and smash. Not delicate, but they weren't going to be hiding much longer anyway. What interested Ghoul more was the existence of this lock at all. She'd been breaking into buildings all day, and it was easily the best defense Ghoul had come across. Who had decided this hidden door in an abandoned building was worth such protection?

Making her way down the stairs, Ghoul passed into the basement where she found the others waiting. Seeing the lock had piqued her curiosity, but there didn't seem to be anything in here worth guarding. Some rusted old tools, scraps of paper wadded up and piled in random spots, a

boiler that clearly hadn't been functional for decades, and…
an axe.

The existence of an axe wasn't surprising in itself, rather the placement made it interesting. Instead of being piled up with the rest of the tools, it was embedded in the middle of the floor. The natural suspicion was that her cohorts had been messing around, but that wasn't the sort of thing Jester tolerated. If the axe was like that, then it was how they'd found it. So why would someone slam an axe into the ground?

"Are we set?" Jester asked. His voice brought Ghoul back to reality, reminding her that they had far more pressing concerns than a curiously stored axe.

"Communications are down. There's a storm front blowing in as well, so hopefully even if they notice, the weather will take the blame," Ghoul reported.

Jester said nothing at first; he was busy slipping his mask back into place. Of them all, none spent more time masked than Jester. He would remove it to live his life and keep up a cover, but in private, he always dwelled beneath the hideous beauty of his mask. Sometimes, Ghoul imagined him relaxing when putting it on, even though she'd never actually seen Jester at ease, not even for a moment. Finally, when the mask was fully donned, he continued.

"Excellent work. Burlap, let's use the storm to our advantage. Wait until there's a round of lightning, then use that as cover to blow the bridge. If we time it well, they could mistake the noise for thunder and blame the loss of a bridge on nature. The longer we keep them off balance, the freer we'll be to make our moves."

Jester strolled over to the axe in the center of the room, idly looking it over. "To think, amateurs earned such a reputation by coming here and chopping a few people up with hastily grabbed equipment. I can only wonder what sort of legends will spring up around the scene we leave behind." Reaching out, he grabbed the axe and pulled, three times, yanking it free from the ground at last on his final tug. For a split-second, Ghoul thought she spotted something on the floor moving, but all she could see was an odd amount of dust spreading across the floor.

"Still, there's no reason not to use a scapegoat when one presents itself. Credit is for amateurs, what matters is the art. And tonight, I suspect Mr. Giggles will be credited with quite the macabre gallery."

Thunder shook the building, near enough that Ghoul could feel the vibrations. Her brow creased, that was fast. She'd come in moments ago, and while there were clouds on the horizon, they'd been a distance off. Maybe the wind was stronger than she knew. Shaking her head, Ghoul removed such silly concerns from her mind.

There was no need to fear something as simple as the weather. They were the scariest things in this park; it was the prey who should be afraid. Once midnight arrived, a storm would be the least of their concerns.

6

The last of the dust joined its brethren, separated so very long ago. Slowly, it slid into place, a form taking shape. The body was tall and thick, honed by years of underpaid and unsafe work keeping an amusement park running. Stained coveralls, once a cheerful light blue, appeared from under the shifting dust, followed soon by weather-beaten patches of skin. Last came the head. Pink and black, singed sections breaking up the light pastel. Two ears, both flopped over, a smiling, half-bemused expression, and painted-on eyes as dead as the man hidden behind them. A pair of heavy boots swung over from the table, setting down heavily onto the wooden floor.

Mr. Giggles rose. At last, the axe was moved, the final piece of his flesh set free. Crackles of electricity ran along his skin, and thunder clapped overhead. Worse, worse by far, were the sounds and stink of people. People in the park. People in *his* park. Mr. Giggles knew where he was, he knew every inch of this place, no matter how it changed or aged. He'd been revived in the old character costume storage room. Sometimes he came back in the midway, sometimes down here, once he'd even awoken atop the coaster where it all began.

His hands flexed involuntarily, reaching for his axe. It was nowhere nearby, and those flexing hands turned into fists. He needed his axe; he wasn't complete without his axe. This wasn't the first time he'd come back without it, though. In fact, it happened more often than not. Stumbling forward, Mr. Giggles put a thick hand against the nearest wall. Through a small corner of unblocked window, he could just make out the final rays of daylight peeking through.

Soon. Soon, he could leave. The storm was coming, the storm always came, but Mr. Giggles was not a creature of the sun. Monsters weren't meant for the daylight, and even in his condition, Mr. Giggles knew to wait the same way he'd been naturally drawn to his axe. He was a creature of pure impulse, driving only by urges and instincts.

Awaken. Find the axe. Kill. KILL. *KILL*. die. Repeat.

When the sun was gone.

Soon.

The peal of thunder drew some mumbled annoyance from the people in suits, but otherwise garnered no major interest. They were more concerned with helping themselves to the expertly crafted catering being served from steaming containers. It looked delicious, unfortunately look was all that Cori and her crew were able to do.

Ajax had provided them with dinner, in that they had food to eat. Staring down the cheap, plastic-wrapped sandwiches was hard to swallow both for culinary reasons, and due to looking at a mountain of nearby shrimp they weren't allowed to touch. All that kept Cori from complaining was the fact that Ajax was eating the same sandwiches as them.

Most of the support staff were, she noted. The fine-dining was only for the executives. The rest were expected to eat what they were given.

Making a mental note to lock down specifics about lodging and dining in her next contract, Cori winced at another clap of thunder. There had been some potential weather warnings, but this was coming in unusually fast. The sky was turning gray and black as the clouds raced the late summer sun to see who could darken the world first. Cori wasn't especially scared of the weather; she was just a realist. They had to get night shots, and a storm would make their job substantially harder. Her best-case scenario at this point was hoping she'd only be running around with lightning to worry about. If rain came too, it all got that much harder.

Between the shifting weather and the horrendous dinner, Cori decided there were better ways to use her time. Closing her eyes, too aware she needed the nutrition and energy, Cori wolfed down the rest of her sandwich, washing it down with a can of discount energy drink. Horace and Bernard both took the cue and increased their own pace. Both were fast eaters anyway, they wouldn't need long.

"If you'll excuse us, I think we'll try and get some night shots as soon as the sun goes down. Since it looks like we're racing a storm, I want to be in position the moment our lighting is right." Cori picked up her bag as she explained things to Ajax, who looked up with an expression of brief worry.

"That... should be fine. There were some activities planned later in the evening, for the executives I mean, that won't be recorded. I'll meet up with you before then to make sure you don't accidentally shoot the wrong footage, but there's nothing to worry about on that front for the next hour and a half. Be in the midway at that time, and I'll guide you to the places you can continue filming."

"Sounds perfect." It sounded like shit, really, however some time free from a handler beat none, so Cori wasn't going to look a gift horse in the mouth. Shooting a glance to Bernard and Horace, she saw both men wiping off the final crumbs from their face and lifting their gear. "We'll try to get as much done before then as possible. Should help us stay out of the executives' way."

Ajax's face visibly relaxed at those words, and Cori knew she'd made the right move. There very well might be a few things she *did* want to film once the night festivities began, but having someone suspicious would only make the job harder.

Until then, she had a lot of shots to get, and no idea when the storm would begin.

7

Mr. Giggles didn't need to wait until midnight. He didn't have to lay plans, or map escape routes, or discern how to best manipulate his prey. This wasn't some weekend warrior camp or rage outlet from his everyday life. There was no everyday life. There was only this endless cycle of blood, pain, and death. Mr. Giggles existed to kill, nothing else. All that kept him from wandering through the countryside, slaying as he went, was the park's limitations.

Once a victim was across that bridge, Mr. Giggles couldn't follow. His feet refused to carry him past the entrance. Whatever magic or curse kept him alive also bound him to this place. Mr. Giggles belonged at Giggletime Mountain, after all. But there were plenty of people above-ground. He could hear them, banging around, traipsing through *his* park. His hands itched for the axe, closing around a handle that wasn't actually there. The last bits of sun had faded from the window, leaving only darkness streaming through. No more waiting. No more soon.

Using the labyrinthine layout of hidden rooms and

tunnels, originally designed so characters could appear and vanish without kids seeing them change, Mr. Giggles made his way out into the windy night. He emerged behind a midway booth where rings and wooden milk bottles were laid out, both warped with time and weather. A new sound reached Mr. Giggles, something other than the looming storm and the intruders.

Splashing. Next to the booth, facing away from Mr. Giggles, was a man wearing an expensive suit. Given his posture, and the sound of liquid hitting canvas, his reason for being here was easy to discern. The axe was the most important thing, but it was an eventual importance, the sort of thing that had to be dealt with even if it wasn't done immediately. If he had to search anyway, Mr. Giggles might as well fulfill his purpose along the way.

Grabbing one of the wooden bottles, Mr. Giggles stood, poised and waiting, for the piss to finish. He could have smashed the man's unwitting head in, but his arm didn't budge. There was a way these things were done. Unfortunately, the gentleman must have been hitting the sauce heavily early on, because he was still producing a substantial stream. Mr. Giggles adjusted his grip, patience waning. The bottle's tip brushed against the tent awning, creating a soft rattle along the metal rings keeping it attached.

Somehow, this penetrated the peeing man's senses. He spun around, stream unstopped, and came face to face with Mr. Giggles. In spite of the solid minute he'd already spent emptying himself, the man's stream increased substantially as a horrid scream escaped his lips, terror washing over someone who was in no way ready to face that horrible burned mask.

Satisfied at last, Mr. Giggles brought the bottle down, caving the man's skull in with a single blow. He added a few more hits, just to be thorough. After a wait like that, he needed to do the first kill right. When there was more pulp than head remaining, Mr. Giggles dropped the milk bottle and walked away from the tent. He stepped to the middle of the midway, lifting his head and giving it a sniff. The air smelled charged, ready, it was the winds just before a storm. This was always the weather, when Mr. Giggles was around. He could smell the source of the charge, too. His axe was deeper in the park, tucked somewhere far away. Before he could find the exact spot, a new smell pressed into his nostrils. Piss. His pants and shoes had been covered by the terrified man's final whizz.

It would fade with time. Until then, Mr. Giggles would track the axe as best he could. If more people were in the way... well, he'd have preferred to do it with his axe, but an amusement park offered no shortage of ways to thin out trespassers.

A new peal of thunder roared overhead, streaks of lightning firing through the sky. Mr. Giggles had arrived, and with him came the storm. Rain may or may not appear for brief stints; that was never the real show. Searing strikes, burning winds, these were the true markings of his storm. The man and the maelstrom were intertwined, connected, bound and trapped in the same cosmic trunk. Besides the axe, the storm was his only constant. Mr. Giggles set off down the midway, concealed only by natural darkness, sniffing as he went. So many intruders between him and his axe.

Perhaps he should have brought along a few milk bottles.

Cori was getting night shots of an old racing game with ramps and pennies when she heard the scream. It wasn't just the volume or intensity that scared her, people ran into terrifying shit all the time in places like this, especially the ones who weren't used to such locations. No, what made the sound scary was its brevity. The scream cut off suddenly, without tapering. As if something had happened to the source.

"Damnit, think somebody found a place to get hurt?" Horace asked.

"That, or they just found out the executive buffet is out of shrimp." Bernard was already grabbing the gear in spite of his snark. He knew the rules for exploring these sorts of locations, and watching out for one another was a foundation of such a practice.

Cori used the handheld camera she was already holding and flicked on its bulb, creating a makeshift flashlight. Leading the team, she wound through the midway, hunting for the source of the sound. For a moment, Cori thought she saw movement further down an aisle, but a sudden new smell brought her up short. It smelled like a bar after one in the morning or a college restroom all the time. Someone had been peeing nearby.

Relief flooded her system as it all clicked into place. Some idiot didn't want to schlep back to the resort bathrooms, so they cut loose out here and probably fell into a hole or some such nonsense. Cutting a far more casual pace, Cori swept her camera around, hunting for the source. When the light fell upon a patch of red, she was confused at first. Then, she came around the corner and saw the rest of the scene.

To her credit, Cori didn't scream. Some of that was because she was forcing her stomach to stay appeased, rather than hurling up the terrible dinner. Most of it, however, was self-preservation. This was no accident; there was a bloody murder weapon right next to the body. A scream meant drawing attention, quite possibly the attention of whoever had done this.

Taking some time to make sure she got a good shot of the body—she was going to need proof to show everyone else—Cori backed away, motioning for Horace and Bernard not to get close. Turning around, she walked up to them, lowering her camera as she did.

"Quickly, and quietly, making no noise and talking to no one else, we need to go back to the hotel. And if I run, be sure you follow."

8

Something was wrong. Something beyond the loud claps of thunder coming more and more frequently, gently rattling their hiding place. Jester made it a point to be aware of every movement and development his prey went through; it was part of being thorough. One aspect of that had entailed slipping listening devices down at a few spots within the park. They were hardly fancy, short-range and homemade, none would last longer than a day, but that was all the team needed. Listening carefully, the earpiece tucked away under his mask, Jester could hardly believe what he heard. Scanning the room, he looked over his people carefully.

A smashed-in head, like what the woman was reporting, would require exceptional strength. Ghoul was out, she was better at precision than brute force. Burlap could have done it, but he never strayed from orders. To say he wouldn't kill someone if needed was preposterous; he just would have let Jester know afterward. That only left Wolf, which was a problem. Wolf might be strong enough, and could be unpredictable at times, but he was terrible at covering evidence. To achieve splatter like what they were describing and walk in here without so much as a speck of blood on his clothes or a shadow of worry in his eyes... either it wasn't Wolf, or the man had been a secret mastermind all along.

No, the team probably hadn't been part of this killing. It simply didn't line up with what Jester saw, and he was a man who trusted his observations. That meant there was another killer here with them. Perhaps it was a crime of passion; maybe they had some true competition. Regardless, this changed things for them significantly.

"Burlap, blow the bridge right now." Wolf and Ghoul looked over to Jester uncertainly, while Burlap took out a device and began hitting switches. That was what Jester liked about Burlap, the man followed orders without hesitation. For the others, he continued explaining. Best they know the new situation.

"Someone has been killed already, head crushed in with an old midway prop. There's a woman trying to report it to security, although they appear to think she's making some kind of ploy. Eventually, they'll take it seriously though, and when that happens we need to be ready. As soon as word gets out, people will try to call for help and find that *all* communications are down, not just cell phones. After that, they'll run for the bridge. Better to take it out now, since the cover is already blown."

Tentatively, Wolf spoke up. "Should we consider bailing instead? If there's another body, they'll know something is up. We won't have surprise on our side anymore. You're always saying we need to work smart."

In a way, Wolf had him. Staying put was not the smart call, strictly speaking. But opportunities like this hunt came along rarely, and plans didn't necessarily have to be scrapped as soon as one element went awry. Besides, they had an easy escape method the moment things got too dangerous. Taking their time and assessing the situation certainly had merit. Jester didn't bother sharing all that with Wolf, however. Most of it would have gone over the man's head. Instead, Jester merely pointed over to Burlap.

"Perhaps, but since Burlap just detonated the only mundane means of escape, we're momentarily stuck here. Once they find both the body and the bridge, panic will set in, making our movements more difficult. All we have to do is wait patiently for opportunities to present themselves. If none do, we'll take our leave when the chaos subsides."

"And what about the other killer?" Ghoul asked. "Planning to just let him run around loose?"

"It depends." Jester hadn't quite decided on that option yet. If it was just some jealous lover or vengeful colleague, then there was no point in getting excited. On the other hand, if their opponent was another professional, this could be interesting. Outside of his recruiting efforts, Jester had never met another person quite like himself. Even his teammates were mere imitations, the best he could scrounge up. Someone else with the vision and ambition to set off on their own, how much fun would *they* be to kill? True, the scene described was grisly and spoke to inexperience; however, a trained specialist could make their murders appear in any way they wanted. People would underestimate a mindless brute, a mistake Jester had no intention of making.

"If we can use this new element to our advantage, we steer clear and let them rampage. If they get in our way, they become just another victim." Jester hefted up the axe from the floor, giving it a quick twirl in his hands. "On the chance we have another copycat, I've even got the perfect weapon to do them in with. Hopefully they have enough taste to appreciate the historical touch."

The pair had snuck off during dinner, making their way into one of the abandoned food stalls. Finding space without dust and cobwebs took work, but having more than a few drinks helped them not to care so much. Together, they found a plastic-covered bench next to a deep-fryer still stocked with spoiled oil. Ripping the cover away revealed simple wood, yet it may as well have been a million-dollar mattress, so glad they were to find a clean surface.

Shirts came off, pants and skirt followed soon. Her purse knocked over, exposing a picture of a smiling husband, perhaps a bit less handsome than he had been before getting sick. The man had no picture of a wife he was betraying; he considered himself single and unattached, although the two kids in different states who'd never met their father might have told him differently. Just as he was reaching for the bra, his companion put a hand on his chest.

"Did you… piss yourself?"

"Wait, what? Why would I do that? I doubt I even could." Glancing down, the man confirmed that he was indeed in a state that would make urinating quite difficult. Yet as he looked, he also sniffed, and there was indeed a noticeable scent in the air. "Oh god, I do smell that though. Must be some kind of animal?"

At his angle, he could only see his companion stiffen as a shadow fell across her face. Whipping around, the man found himself face-to-face with a pink rabbit head that had been charred black in several places. Reaching out, the behemoth grabbed the deep-fryer, sparks flying from his hand and lighting up the machine. He flipped it on top of them, pinning both. The oil, formerly sludge, was starting to heat up somehow, even though there was no way the machine should be running. A thick, oozing drop slipped out, splattering on the floor.

The pinned man's eyes went wide as he watched the rabbit-headed monster take a container of old oil and dump it all over them, as well as the fryer keeping the couple pinned to the bench. From nearby, he took a box of matches, lighting one with the first strike. There was barely enough time for the couple to scream before the match fell, but they managed it all the same.

Seconds later, there was only the burning food stall lighting up the night, casting a floppy-eared shadow of the man slowly walking away.

9

Thick, slamming waves roamed the water, like a pack of muggers hunting for some unsuspecting soul they could force below the surface. Despite the lack of rain, there was definitely a storm rolling through, with enough wind to stir up the river even worse than normal. On top of that, it was clearly raining somewhere, because the speed of the current had increased substantially. None of which should have been a problem, since they were planning to drive right over it.

Unfortunately, the chunks of concrete still occasionally splashing down below betrayed the issue: there was now a serious gap between the bridge and the amusement park. If someone was very athletic and feeling extremely confident, they might be able to leap across, but if they failed they were in for the swim of a lifetime. Probably very literally.

"The storm must have messed up the bridge." Ajax had rejoined them, thrust onto the team after they reported finding a dead body. Most likely, the higher-ups were worried about Cori and her team causing trouble, but in truth, she was glad for the addition. The film hadn't been as high quality as she was hoping, making it hard to convince everyone with footage alone. Once they checked the actual scene, accusations and suspicion would start flying. Having an alibi generator with her at all times wasn't the worst situation for an outsider, especially one who'd found a corpse. That assumed there would be more trouble, of course, and as Cori stared out at the churning waves, her gut told her that was definitely in the cards.

"You think a storm did this? The river is high, but it's not *that* high, and the kind of wind you'd need to tear it up would have knocked us down before we came near this close. Maybe a lightning strike could be viable, if there were scorch marks or any other sign of them along the remaining concrete. As it stands, the storm is just about the only entity I can say with certainty isn't responsible for this." Bernard had a camera in hand as he spoke, dutifully recording all that lay before them. The man was a professional, on top of his tech expertise.

Despite the calm tones, Ajax still gulped visibly. "You're saying someone else did this?"

"Bernard can be a little rough around the edges," Horace said, stepping in with a reassuring smile. "He's just saying the storm didn't cause this. There are still plenty of other, non-panic inducing explanations."

From further back in the amusement park, Cori caught the sound of screams. When she turned her head, a plume of smoke, thin and already fading, was rising through the sky. This was an old park, accidents happened, a fire didn't necessarily mean… no, that was self-delusion. She was in danger, if not from a killer then from a deeply defective park, and ignoring that wouldn't make them any safer. Part of exploring dangerous locales meant accepting the truth as it was and moving forward. It was the only way to keep a cool head, and they would need clear thinking in a situation like this.

"Okay, so the bridge is down, one person got their head smashed in, and it sure looks like something behind us caught fire. If we were to entertain the idea that another Mr. Giggles has shown up to kill everyone, what would the next move be? My cell still has no bars, and so far as I know this was the only way off of here."

"You… you could try scaling the cliff to the west." Ajax was breathing heavily, his pale skin gleaming with sweat. This was probably a lot more than he'd been expecting to deal with. "But it's steep and sheer. The park had to install multiple safety fences after some people tumbled down in the first year. Probably hasn't gotten better."

Bernard was testing his own cell, finding it as useless as Cori's. "What about a landline? This place is old, so they must have had some."

That seemed to calm Ajax, albeit slightly. "Right, there are landlines at every major building. All we have to do is reach one, and we can call for help."

Racing back into a park where fires and bodies were appearing was hardly Cori's favorite nighttime activity, but it beat standing in the open with nowhere to run except into raging waters. Besides, if they happened to get a shot of the new Mr. Giggles, the video would essentially make itself viral. The numbers and quality of their offers would shoot up significantly. Still, Cori found herself hoping she walked out of this night with as little video as possible. Meeting a serial killer wouldn't be worth it, no matter how desirable the shot.

"Horace, you've got the best memory for our locations. What's the nearest major building?" Cori asked.

Rubbing the back of his neck, Horace looked out at the dark park. "From the layouts we studied, there's a building not too far off that houses the entrances and consoles for three rides. While there's no guarantee they would have a phone, it's on our way back to the hotel anyway. We can skip it and run back to the rooms, or roll the dice and see what they've got. Your call, boss."

More noise was coming from the park, and it sure sounded like people screaming. Could be from the fire, could be they'd found the smashed head of their coworker, or it could be other reasons. Being on their own was risky, but Cori had little faith in the sense of a panicking crowd. At least Ajax was keeping it semi-together, and she trusted her team not to buckle so easily.

"The faster, the better. Besides, there's bound to be someone at the hotel trying the phones. Let's swing by the other building first. Even if it's redundant, it beats standing around like this, wondering what to do. Horace, lead the way."

They cut a brisk pace away from the churning waves, still swirling and inviting any who felt daring to come dance in their cold depths. In a way, the river was merciful. True, it offered death, yet at least it would be a relatively swift one. Compared to some of the killings Giggletime Mountain had borne witness too, the idea of a quick death could be seen as downright merciful.

The time for hiding was at an end. Although the presence of an intruder had certainly sped up their timetable, Jester felt no anger at the interloper. Surprises and coping with the unexpected were part of this lifestyle; if Jester were not prepared for such things, then the failing would be his. Such was not the case, as he led the others along a shadowy aisle that had once held an array of shops stocked with over-priced souvenirs.

From not too far off, they could hear the shouts and yells of their prey. With one body already in play, it wasn't hard to figure out what they would discover at the source of the flames. After that, it would be a predictable slide into chaos and panic as the thin veneer of civilization slipped away, revealing the animals lurking beneath. Accusations would fly, old grudges and suspicions would be unearthed, by the night's end they might well kill more of one another out of fear than what Jester's team could ever hope to manage. Humans were such pointless, predictable creatures. They lacked the capacity to surprise, or at least to surprise someone like Jester.

In a sense, that was where this had all started. Supposedly, in a crisis, the greater part of the human soul was said to emerge. Courage, honor, brave heroics, the sorts of things most of this chaff would be incapable of in a given day. Jester had wanted to see if the lowly truly did have it them to be better when a situation turned dire. Thus far in his experiments, there was no such luck. Sometimes there were brave ones, of course, but they had shown such traits beforehand. It was the surprise, the ability to break free from one's own character, that Jester had wanted to witness. Luckily enough, the experiments had proved entertaining in other ways, and a new passion was kindled.

"Can we set up in the haunted house first?" Wolf asked. "I'd really like to get some of those while the crowd is thick."

Jester opted not to visibly bristle at the words; Wolf had managed to keep his volume in check this time, so chastising him could send the wrong message. "That decision belongs to Ghoul. With the new situation, do you think you can still lure people in?"

She took her time responding, giving the situation proper contemplation. "I think I can swing it, but I can't promise how many I'll pull at once. Also, I'm going to need Burlap's help."

"In the haunted house, numbers will have little meaning. The array of paths, not to mention the employee passages we found on the blueprints, will permit us freedom of movement. Short of drawing the entire company at once, we should be able to handle however many you can bring." Jester swept the axe through the air once, enjoying the feel of it in his hands. While not normally a fan of specific tools, this one had a nice weight. He might even have to break his rule about not taking souvenirs.

Blinking, Jester took a step back from that last thought. He was considering breaking one of his most fundamental rules for a simple axe? How preposterous. Yet at the thought of setting the weapon down, his whole body balked. Something was amiss here, an element he'd yet to discern. Rather than being bothered, Jester felt the closest thing to joy he was capable of.

Perhaps tonight would have a few surprises in store after all.

* * *

Mr. Giggles jammed the sleeve of cotton candy cones deeper into his victim's throat, eliciting a half-choked gurgle before the balding man slumped over, clearly dead. Another kill, yet he was no closer to his axe. Tilting his head back, he gave a tentative sniff. Mostly, it just stank of piss thanks to the stains on Mr. Giggles' clothing, but he could still catch a few whiffs of the axe. Up until now, it had been in one direction. The scent had shifted during his last kill, though. It was moving, back toward the section with walking attractions.

Whoever had his axe also possessed good taste. Mr. Giggles had killed many a soul in that area. Tonight, it seemed he would add a few more to the count. Steadily, leaving the body behind, he began traipsing off toward the thieves who would pay for taking his weapon.

* * *

"Help me!" The voice came from a set of dark buildings, breaking up the casual chatter of the bankers. They'd skipped out on the post-dinner socializing, instead opting to sneak off somewhere that they wouldn't need to share any of their designer drugs. All talk of plans for their next luxury sex tour of a third-world nation were scrapped as they caught sight of a beautiful woman bolting from the shadows. Her clothing was ripped in a few strategic places, but it hadn't given up the ghost quite yet. "Please, hurry, I need help!"

Several steps behind her, a hulking man wearing a burlap sack over his head stepped into view. He reached down, grabbing the woman by the arms. In spite of his size, she was able to put up a fight, yanking her limbs away as she looked over to them, lovely eyes wide and pleading. "Save me!"

That shook them out of their reverie, snapping into motion. True, the man was big, but they had the advantage of numbers, plus if that slip of a woman could hold him off he clearly wasn't that strong. Unfortunately, just as they sprang into action, the kidnapper managed a blow to the woman's head, knocking her unconscious. He half-carried, half-dragged the now limp lady back into the shadows, managing to disappear through the entrance of a haunted house before the group arrived.

"Do we keep chasing?"

"Did you *see* that chick? Fuck yeah we chase. Wouldn't mind her owing me some gratitude, and that big bastard could barely move her. We'll take them in no time."

Some of it was bravado, a *lot* of it was cocaine, regardless, with absolute confidence the bankers all plunged through the door, giving themselves over to the haunted house.

The décor of the haunted house had once been cheesy, but years of rotting and negligence had accomplished what an underpaid summer intern couldn't: making this place genuinely unsettling. Wallpaper was curling down from the ceiling, dust covered near every surface, and various decayed props littered the area, making it impossible to know what was real and what was trash. Pulling out their cell phones, the men lit up the dark interior. Even if there was no coverage here, those thousand-dollar devices made decent substitute flashlights.

There were several different routes they could take, stairs to the left, a hall to the right, and what appeared to be a cracked open door in front of them. One of the few whose minds wasn't entirely lost in the cocaine blizzard had enough sense to look down for footprints in the dust. Nothing there.

"Fuuuuck. Guys, did we hallucinate that whole thing?" He turned to find the others already sprinting off, none of them in a mental place where standing around and talking felt like a good move. Seeing them scatter, this one opted to try the door right before them. Once he cleared the room, he could follow the others, or just leave and do another bump. Probably the second one, with the woman out of sight he was having trouble thinking all this was worth the effort.

Shoving open the door, he found himself staring at a huge mechanical vampire, half the plastic of its face warped and drooping. It must have been intended to spring out and scare guests, but whatever mechanisms were in place had long ago failed, or there wasn't even power being supplied to this section of the park. The monster did give him a start, which was why it took him several seconds to notice the pain in his neck. Like a bug bite, only worse. As he slid to the ground, his vision shifted, giving him a look at an alcove just behind the door where a man in a cheap werewolf mask had been hiding. While one hand moved the door back to its original position, the other held an empty syringe. A last drop of green liquid splashed down from the needle to the floor.

"Now don't you worry, that's just going to keep you nice and still while I have my fun—holy shit!" Wolf's terrifying speech was immediately cut off as the businessman he'd injected began to spasm and convulse. The serum shouldn't have done that; the only time they'd seen anything like this was when someone had other drugs in their system. Looking closer, Wolf noted the dusting of white around the nostrils. Blood trickled out from the man's lips, and just like that the convulsions ended.

He was dead, and that was the goal, but it had been somewhat lackluster for Wolf's tastes. They were supposed to be able to enjoy themselves, and Ghoul was expecting him to bring her a victim since she'd been tasked with bait-duty. The woman was not forgiving when disappointed.

New sounds came from outside, fresh footsteps. Working fast, Wolf dragged the corpse out of the way and readied his next syringe. Using more drugs was a risk, but Jester would far prefer dead bodies to someone living long enough to raise a ruckus. Disappointing Ghoul was scary, disappointing Jester was not fucking happening. Needle in hand, Wolf waited, hoping the newcomer would wander into his trap.

Sniffing, his face pinched. Had the businessman pissed himself in the convulsions? It sure stank of whizz in here all of a sudden.

***

Dust rose from the floor at Mr. Giggles' heavy steps. From his shoulders, sparks flew when they came too close to the wiring. Lights began to flicker dimly, the few bulbs that had any life left to give, and a very slow recording of a witch cackle started playing, the reduced speed making it far more unsettling than the original. His axe was here. He could smell it. This close, he could practically feel it. Where though? That was the question. Mr. Giggles was not a creature of tactical consideration, there was only one way he knew to search: one room at a time, piece by piece.

He slammed through the doorway, coming face to face with the sagging-faced vampire. At his proximity, more sparks few, and one of the vampire's eyes lit up. The jaw began lower, exposing a pair of metal fangs with fading paint and a mouth that showed exposed wires if one looked deep enough. A force pushed on Mr. Giggles' neck, and he turned around to find a man in a werewolf mask holding some kind of needle.

Behind him was a corpse, with blood running from its mouth. Mr. Giggles didn't remember killing this one. Mr. Giggles never forgot a murder. Someone else had done the deed, and without any showmanship whatsoever. Movement grabbed his attention, the werewolf was backpedaling now.

"Holy shit, there really is another copycat. Listen, man, sorry about the syringe. How about instead of torture, I take you to the boss while it wears off? I bet he'd love to chat with you."

Mr. Giggles did not like this man. Killing in his park was bad enough. Killing this way, practical over theatrical, was blasphemy. Without a word, he reached down and grabbed the werewolf by his shoulder, heaving the small man up without effort.

"Hey. Hey! What the fuck! How about some professional courtesy, you sack of shit?"

Mr. Giggles ignored the rising squeals. Instead, he grabbed the werewolf's head, pulling it back to expose the throat. With a forceful slam, he drove that neck up into the exposed vampire fangs, gouging deep into the werewolf's throat. There was screaming, as usual, but it soon turned to gurgling. Using uncharacteristic delicacy, Mr. Giggles set the werewolf down atop the vampire's outstretched arms.

Blood ran from the throat, creating a growing puddle on the floor. Mr. Giggles admired the work before he left the room. He could still feel the axe; there was more searching to do. And potentially, more pretenders to vanquish.

1 2

Everything was in position for a nice, long session when the screams reached Jester's ears. He knew Wolf's voice, and saw no reason to pretend it wasn't the one he'd just heard. Something had gone wrong. If it was going to happen to anyone, it would happen to Wolf. This left them with a precarious decision to make. Should they be caught, they could likely deal with the discoverers, but it wasn't certain. Especially not with another killer on the loose. Jester decided that this early in the night, discretion served them better than aggression.

"Liquate." Jester said the word once, before taking one of Ghoul's knives and slitting the throat of his prey, a gentleman in a fine suit who was tied to a chair.

Following his command, Ghoul and Burlap dispatched the others who had been waiting for their turn in the chair. Without pausing, save only long enough for Jester to scoop up the axe, they slipped into a passageway. It curved through the building, spitting them out a hidden backdoor partially blocked off by debris. Within a minute of hearing the scream, Jester's entire team was free.

Now came the crossroads. If he went back to check on Wolf, Jester would risk discovery, but it was too dangerous to chance leaving him. Wolf knew too much, and he lacked the inner conviction of the others. Under torture, he would eventually crack and give the operation up. Jester couldn't allow that. Given that all he had to work on was a scream, it was worth the danger of going back to confirm what happened to his asset. That didn't mean he had to go in foolishly, however.

Jester removed his mask and the plastic smock keeping blood from his clothes. He handed both of these items and, after a moment of hesitation, the axe over to Burlap. "Stay hidden. I'll handle Wolf."

Slinking back around, Jester now looked like nothing more than another random person here for the event. He slipped in to the front of the haunted house, skipping the hidden entrance Burlap and Ghoul had used and proceeding to the main foyer. It was odd that some of the lights were blinking, and a few of the speakers crackled with life. This building shouldn't have any power at all, yet the proof was right in front of Jester's eyes.

There something else before him as well: Wolf. The door had been left open, making the scene impossible to miss. His corpse was draped across the arms of a vampire, neck turning into a ravaged, bloody mess that made a good match for the gruesome fangs above him. Someone went to all the trouble of making it look like a vampire had killed the werewolf. While it was not the same style that Jester himself embraced, he could still appreciate the dedication in another's art.

And this *was* art, no doubt about it. Using the environment, packaging the classic enemies together in a fateful scene, there was classic sense to the spectacle, evoking the very legends that made this amusement park infamous.

Interesting. Jester had always pursued his own style unerringly, seeking to hone and perfect the craft. Whereas this killer clearly adapted, incorporating the lore of their location into the methods. Even if they did turn out to be a copycat, at least they were endeavoring to stay true to the original's spirit.

Noise came from overhead, steps on the floor above, breaking the spell Jester had fallen under. From his pocket, he produced a bottle of accelerant. No plan went perfectly, and when it came time to cover one's tracks, few things were as cleaning as fire. Wolf was lost, which was inconvenient, but they couldn't permit his death to compromise their operation. Dousing the body with clear liquid, Jester lingered only long enough to strike a match and throw it on Wolf's body.

Immediately, it began to burn, which Jester took as a cue to leave. He didn't need much convincing anyway; now that he was done appreciating the scene, Jester had begun to catch the stink of urine lingering in the room. Noticing a dead businessman in the corner as he left, Jester realized the man must have lost his bowels in death. It was fortunate that pee was the worst of the smells.

Heading back into the night, Jester joined the others, reclaiming his mask, smock, and axe. The last one caused him to shiver slightly as he took it back. Unwillingly, his eyes went up, to the second floor of the haunted house. There, through a window barely big enough to fit a person's head, was a shape staring down from the shadows, looking at him. It was too dark to make out many features, yet those floppy ears were too distinct to miss.

Hands slammed on the glass, and an inhuman howl burst forth. Jester was not a man of fear; however, he did understand prudence's importance. Much as he might like to meet the fellow artist, this was clearly not the occasion. Something was amiss; Wolf had probably tried to strike and angered this agent of death. Better to wait until tempers cooled and they could have a more productive discussion.

"Move." Jester darted into the night, taking it as a given that Burlap and Ghoul would follow. They did, neither bothering to ask what happened to Wolf. Each one could already see the smoke beginning to drift out of the haunted house as the fire spread. They knew the fate that awaited them, if they should fall. This hadn't always been the team composition. Others had come before. Others would come after Ghoul and Burlap were the ones burning. Only Jester was constant. Death was the cost of living, for however long, in his presence.

But it wasn't a cost either was ready to pay yet. Especially not with such an interesting night ahead of them. It had been a long while since they saw anyone take Jester by surprise. Seeing him set against a real adversary, that was a sight worth living long enough to witness.

13

Getting to the ride building took longer than it should have. Were it a simple walk, they'd have arrived in a few minutes, but the throngs of panicking people slowed their progress substantially. Corpses and fires popping up on what was supposed to be a fun outing had shaken this group to its core. The high-powered business people were collectively losing their shit; being faced with a real problem outside of which car to take to the foreclosure meetings had forced many into an ugly realization: they had no inner strength to lean on. Consequentially, they were all fast losing any grip on societal rules and sanity. Some had stripped their jackets off, wrapping them around old timber into makeshift torches, while others collapsed in place, crying and defecating as they rocked.

Cori was relieved when they finally reached the building, a squat bunker situated between several attractions, the spoke in the wheel that kept things turning. As they approached, she caught sight of a small detail through her lens and held up a hand to slow the others. "That door is open."

Normally, they'd ignore such a triviality, but with a killer on the loose that was a red flag that had to be heeded. Of course, that didn't mean they could just walk away either. If the murderer was in there, there could also be another victim, or a person about to fill that role. Horace took the front position while Bernard grabbed the rear, shifting Cori and Ajax between them. Neither had a weapon, but both produced the heaviest camera on their person. Using an incredibly expensive instrument as a club would certainly suck, yet it still beat dying by a substantial margin.

Together, the group entered the door, which led to a stairwell. Moving as softly as they could manage, they ascended. As they went higher, sound reached their ears. A voice, muttering to itself, cursing softly. Horace was the first to reach the next floor and see the source, with Cori right on his heels. It was not a murderer, or not someone blatantly showing off an intent to kill, anyway. Instead, they found the woman who had driven them over the bridge fiddling with the wiring of the landline phone.

"Come on, you piece of shit, everything is connected right, why aren't you working?" She wasn't paying attention to them; her entire focus was on the half-disassembled phone. Unsure of how else to break the silence, Cori looked to her friends and made sure they were ready for whatever came next.

"Um, ma'am, what are you doing?"

The driver shot up so fast she clipped her head on a shelf, cracking the wood and drawing whispered curses as she rubbed her scalp. "Sweet Jesus, don't sneak up on me like that. There's a damn killer on the loose."

She sounded very confident about that, more than Cori was sure she felt comfortable with. "We saw the body too, that's why we came here looking for a phone."

"Unfortunately, none of them seem to be working." The

driver finished rubbing her head and got to her feet, wiping off her hands on her coveralls as she did. "Tried the hotel one first, dead. Then hit a shop I know, also dead. After finding this one busted too, I have to conclude that something happened to our phone lines."

"Maybe the storm knocked them out?" Ajax suggested.

Behind him, Bernard offered up a slow, condescending pat to the man's shoulder. "Notice how we didn't see any on the way up here? In places like this, they usually bury the lines, meaning a storm shouldn't have messed with anything. Must have been our murderer."

"No, Mr. Giggles doesn't work… like… that…" The driver trailed off as she noticed the sudden increase in scrutiny amongst the people staring at her. "What? You were talking about the legends on the way up here, it's common knowledge."

"I don't recall any of those tales talking about the land-lines," Horace pointed out. "And we did real research for this. Yet you sound pretty damn sure, after we found you messing with a phone."

The accusation, unspoken yet clear, hung in the air. With an inscrutable expression, the driver looked them all over, one at a time. "Fine. You want the truth; I'll give it to you, but don't waste my time asking me to prove any of it. I can't. If I could, my life would have ended up very differently. Besides, we don't have much time. To keep it simple: I know how Mr. Giggles works because I survived his last attack. My name is Tabitha, although most people call me Tabby. I killed Mr. Giggles last time he rose."

"You mean you killed the last ˙copycat pretending to be Mr. Giggles, right?" Ajax was starting to sweat, his eyes taking on a glassy shine similar to the people they'd passed on the way here.

"I said what I meant." Tabby gave the phone one final

glance over before giving it up as a lost cause. "The stories are true, or true enough to be right about the unkillable murderer. No matter what you try, guns, knives, explosions, nothing stops him. His only weakness is his own axe. With that, you can hurt him, and if you leave it in his heart he'll stay dead. For a time. Of course, getting it away from him is half the battle. I was hoping to get everyone evacuated before dealing with that bastard, but fortune must really be against us tonight."

Cori shook her head. "I don't know. There's a murderer on the loose, and we've managed to avoid running into him despite being stuck in the same location. Feels like a lucky break to me."

"Then cross your fingers and kiss a leprechaun, you'll need all the luck you can get to make through the night." Tabby was stowing her tools now, tossing them in a bag that looked much older than her. "There is good news. If you last until sunrise, he goes into hiding. He also can't leave the park, so if you escape then you're good. None of which helps us currently, but at least there's hope should we live to daylight. Now, anyone who wants to help me, come along. Anyone who thinks I'm a crazy van driver, feel free to take your chances on your own. Make a choice now, because I'm not sitting around waiting to be discovered."

She paused, tilting her head back and sniffing. "Also, maybe grab a wet nap or some perfume, because somebody here really stinks like piss."

1 4

The hiss of engine brakes caught everyone's attention. From the south side of the building, a roller coaster car eased into the building, coming to a halt along a section of rusty tracks. Nearly everyone there just stared at it, confused at how a rundown piece of equipment could be suddenly active. Tabby, conversely, sprang into action. She yanked out a huge wrench from her bag and started backing away slowly.

"Everyone, stay calm. Mr. Giggles is nearby. The park comes alive around him, always has. If the car came from the south, then that's his direction too. Quickly, without running, get out of here and make your way to the crowds. He'll chase a target until they're dead, but he prefers the ones who run, and he likes to kill stragglers rather than deal with crowds. Doesn't mean he won't, just a preference."

The rest of the room was looking to one another, uncertain how seriously to take all of this. Then, they heard it. Footsteps. Big, heavy, lumbering footsteps coming from the maintenance tunnel that ran alongside the coaster. Whether it was really a supernatural murderer or not, *someone* was killing people, and this seemed plenty foreboding enough to read as danger. Cori and the others backed their way to the stairs, the same way they'd gone down. She tried to hang back and make her team go first, but only Ajax took the opportunity. Bernard simply planted his feet, while Horace took the time to shake his head and explain.

"Bosses go first. If you fight us, you only waste our time."

It wasn't worth the battle, so Cori headed down, followed by Horace. Bernard was the last one at the top, camera still running. Just as he was turning, their equipment man halted suddenly. His eyes and lens were locked across the room, staring at something no one else could make out. Slowly, Bernard moved the camera, holding it toward the stairs for several seconds before throwing the device to Horace. When he spoke, it was a projected whisper out the side of his mouth, never looking toward them.

"He's looking at me. Right at me. We met eyes. I don't think he can see any of you at this angle. No axe, so I guess Tabby was full of shit after all. I think… I think she was right about one thing though. He's waiting for me to move. To run. I tried to get good footage. Make sure you use it, okay?"

"Wait, Bernard, what are you—"

"Shut up!" Bernard snapped at Horace. "Do you want him to hear you? Look, I'm going to run in another direction. Get out of here, and stay near a crowd. If I get away, I'll find you." With every word, he was tightening the straps on his equipment, making sure it would slow him down as little as possible. "And if I don't… well, I'll keep my bodycam running. Even if he's not magic, video of a murderer right before he kills me is bound to be worth some prizes. Get my name added posthumously."

That was all the warning before Bernard took off in another direction. Instantly, they could make out thundering footsteps giving pursuit. He'd been right; the killer wanted him to run, to make it a chase. All they could hear were the sounds of running, a door slamming, and for a moment, Horace caught sight of a single pink ear. The sight sent a shiver down his spine.

"We need to move," Cori told him. "Bernard has good stamina to lug that shit around all the time. He can escape, so we should do the same." The look on her face made it obvious that not even she was sure whether or not to believe the words. In the end, it didn't matter. Bernard had just raced off on his own, presumed killer in tow. If they wanted that act to matter, then they needed to survive. Long enough to find him, or failing that, avenge him.

Finally looking away from the top of the stairwell, Horace nodded. "Let's go find a crowd."

B ernard could hear the bunny-faced man storming along behind him. He ran without thought, bolting for the first door in his line of sight, which led to a ramp that dumped him out on the northwest side of the building. If not for the noise of his pursuer, it would have been easy to feel safer outdoors, but instead Bernard only ran harder.

He was in an older area of the amusement park, filled with minor rides, attractions, and a large carousel planted right in the center of the section. Bernard chanced a look over his shoulder. The sound of Mr. Giggles was still heavy in the air, as was the smell of piss, weirdly. Visually, Bernard had lost the murderer in a small fake village of plastic cartoon characters. Taking advantage of the brief opportunity, Bernard dashed over to the carousel, hunkering down behind a gray mare. Since it was circular, theoretically he could move with Mr. Giggles, staying out of sight until he lost interest. That was a best-case scenario, admittedly, but

Bernard needed to catch his breath regardless. If nothing else, time to rest might give him enough oxygen for the next sprint.

Unfortunately, the problem with paying such focused attention in one direction was that it made one more vulnerable from other approaches. Bernard didn't even notice the sounds of the approach, although in fairness these footsteps were substantially quieter than those of Mr. Giggles. He felt a strong hand suddenly grab him by the neck and spin him around, showing him three masked faces. The biggest one of them, wearing a burlap sack, was the one holding him in place.

"Do we play?" The voice came from a woman in a truly hideous mask, to a man in some sort of ceramic clown face.

"No time. The real fun is nearly here." With a casual swing, the clown-masked one swept an axe through the air. Bernard felt a brief flash of pain, then warmth, then cold into nothingness as the blood rushed from his neck.

Burlap dropped the corpse as Mr. Giggles finally came into view from around the cartoon village. At his side, Jester let out a noise none of them had heard before. Excitement? Did Jester even have the capacity for that?

"It fills my heart with joy to meet an artist of your caliber," Jester announced, stepping into clear view for Mr. Giggles, axe still in hand. "And I can scarcely contain myself when I imagine the depths of happiness I will know when I spread your organs across the ground."

Whether it was the words or the sight of his kill being stolen, Mr. Giggles wasted no time. He broke into a charge on a direct course with Jester.

15

The plan was simple. Plans had to be simple, in situations this chaotic. Those were the only kind with even a half-decent shot of working. Jester drew Mr. Giggles' attention, Burlap and Ghoul swept in to injure him, then Jester could take his time enjoying the rest. They'd have done anything Jester asked already, but the chance to get revenge for Wolf had both extra keyed up. Even if he'd been the worst of them, he'd still been one of theirs. While death was a risk of the job, that didn't mean either had to be forgiving.

There was no concern or grace in Mr. Giggles' movements. The masked man blundered forward without any apparent care for his surroundings or safety. Ghoul sneered under her mask; this idiot was even worse than Wolf. He didn't deserve the honor of killing one of their team, and she would never let him draw close to Jester. Coming up on his left, from within the carousel, she drove a pair of knives into his leg, cutting vital tendons.

Mr. Giggles did miss a step, stumbling slightly. He didn't collapse the way Ghoul was expecting, however. All he did was slam a powerful arm into Ghoul, sending her sprawling back onto the carousel, bruising her back on a horse as she landed. Mercifully, the distraction had been enough for Burlap to get in position. Their own big man buried a shoulder in Mr. Giggles' torso, lifting him up and driving him onto the carousel as well. It was all Ghoul could do to get clear before they came crashing down.

Small flashes of light, sparks maybe, crackled along Mr. Giggles' back wherever he touched the carousel's floor. To her surprise, Ghoul saw the bulbs flickering on. Soft calliope notes reached her ears only seconds before the ride began to turn, slowly at first, gradually picking up speed.

Had they hit a switch? No, that was crazy, even if there was a button on the floor, this ride wasn't even supposed to have power. But crazy or not, the damn thing was moving, so Ghoul had to accept that fact and deal with it. The carousel was really the least of her current problems.

Mr. Giggles, recovered from the surprise, was getting to his feet. That wouldn't have been so worrying, except that Burlap was trying to knock him down, raining blows on the bunny-headed man's back. Strikes that would have sent normal men to the hospital were completely ignored as Mr. Giggles rose back to standing height. Burlap went back to the one method that had worked, a full-on charge.

This time, unfortunately, Mr. Giggles was ready for it. He caught the huge man with both hands, swinging Burlap around by the shoulders and flinging him into the rising and falling horses behind them. Old wood shattered as Burlap's bulk snapped the top of several poles, knocking some horses to the floor while others continued prancing, just skewed at awkward angles. They shouldn't still be able to work like that, but then again none of it should be working at all, so Ghoul was splitting hairs to focus on such details.

Instead of wondering how this all could happen, she took

advantage of Mr. Giggles leaving his back exposed, slamming a blade through his spine. It should have sent him sprawling, instead it earned her an elbow to the skull that left the world spinning. Ghoul stumbled back, trying to get a grip on herself as her legs wobbled, threatening to betray her. Staying upright took all the effort she had, which meant Ghoul was unable to help as Mr. Giggles turned back to Burlap.

With seemingly no effort, Mr. Giggles grabbed Burlap's substantial form and hefted it overhead. This was beyond strong, this was... supernatural. For the first time in a very long while, since she'd found Jester in fact, Ghoul found herself considering the possibility that the world was bigger than she realized. Believing in magic, in things like souls, seemed so ridiculous when she'd taken dozens of humans apart without ever seeing even a hint of such a thing. Yet, with the carousel's movement and Mr. Giggles' strength, there was no escaping the truth that something strange was going on.

She might have pondered it longer, had there been time. Instead, Ghoul was forced to watch as Mr. Giggles brought Burlap down on top of one of the fractured poles. His aim was faultless, the makeshift stake bursting up through the middle of Burlap's chest, chunks of his heart lodged in the wood. The large man struggled briefly, then went still.

Just when Ghoul was about to taste real fear, Jester appeared, reminding her why the team never worried, no matter how bad things got. Leaping out from around the corner, Jester drove the axe into Mr. Giggles' back as he was stepping away from Burlap. Unlike the knife strikes, this did get a reaction, and a hell of one at that. Mr. Giggles let out an monstrous scream of pain as sparks flew between him and the axe, causing him to stumble forward. Jester, never one to show mercy on a weakened opponent, swung again, aiming for a leg.

The blow missed only because Mr. Giggles stepped back at the right moment. He was slower now, visibly weakened. Ghoul wasn't the only one who knew it, either. Mr. Giggles grabbed the center of the carousel, ripping off a mirrored panel and flinging it toward Jester, who deftly stepped aside. Mr. Giggles wasn't done yet, while Jester was dodging, he wrapped his arms around the rusted metal pillar in the machinery's center and yanked hard to the side.

Immediately, they heard the crack, followed by snaps and pings as the structural integrity of the entire carousel began to give way. Chunks of the ceiling, and all the beams running to the horse's poles, came down near Ghoul's feet. Moving largely on instinct, head still ringing, she staggered her way off of the carousel, ignoring the sounds of destruction coming from all around.

When her vision finally cleared, Ghoul could make out the remains of the ride, and Jester standing nearby, axe in hand. "Did he escape?"

"He brought down the entire carousel just to buy enough time to run, vanishing almost like magic. Yes, he escaped, and he certainly earned it. It was a pity to lose Burlap, but at least he was useful to the very end." Jester turned the axe in his hands, running a thumb carefully along the wooden shaft. "After ignoring attacks from both you and Burlap, he took off the moment I hit him with this. Our killer has a weakness, and it is in our hands."

"So what do we do next?" Ghoul asked. Leaving wasn't up for discussion—so few things interested Jester, when one did she knew he would chase it as long as required.

"Next, we torch the carousel and Burlap's body. After that, we go find more people," Jester replied. "I have an idea, and it requires bait."

16

Things were going downhill, fast. Panic had died off; with nowhere to run the visitors had worn themselves out within the first hour. After that, the weariness of their bodies and the impossibility of the situation left them in a hedonistic mood. People were ducking off behind tents, into hidden nooks and alcoves, some removing clothing, other pulling out bags of illegal substances.

In other circumstances, Cori would have been impressed that all the suit-and-tie folks managed to put on an impromptu Burning Man. As it stood, everywhere she looked, all she could see were potential murder targets. It was taking everything she had not to go hunting for Bernard. Next to her, Horace was trying his cell phone even though there was still no signal, punching in the number anyway and hoping for a miracle.

Seeing a man still clad in his professional attire, without any smoke or powders on him, Cori raced over and grabbed him by the lapel. "We have to get everyone organized! There's a killer on the loose."

"No shit there's a killer on the loose." He stared down at

Cori with the same distaste the suits had used when looking at all the help. "And we're pretty organized already. You're the girl with the lube, right?"

"Huh?" She stared at him, unable to process the words, until another woman appeared. This one looked as professional as her male counterpart, only she was carrying around a sizable bottle of clear liquid.

Walking up, she clapped the man on the shoulder and held up the bottle. "Had to fight off Sanderson, but I got the last bottle. You guys go nuts. I'm off to find the mushrooms."

"Follow the music," her colleague recommended, turning away from Cori without another glance. "They always put on some techno shit when taking the fungus express; I think I can hear it already."

The pair walked off, leaving Cori, Horace, and Ajax all standing there, dumbfounded. Somehow, they had expected some level of survival instinct or competency from the others, which was their own mistake, really. This was not the sort to turn to when any manner of fortitude, be it mental or practical, was required. It was just them against a supposedly supernatural killer who might have already gotten their friend.

"Okay... okay, so they're useless." Cori forced herself to take some deep breaths, thinking the situation through. "We can't count on anyone to help. If Tabitha was right, then the murderer holes up after sunrise, and even if she was wrong it's going to be harder to sneak around butchering people in broad daylight. Surviving until morning has to be our goal."

"Doable. Very doable," Ajax chimed in. "If we blockade ourselves in one of the rooms, we would have a very minimal chance of running into the murderer. Especially with so many other, easier targets out here on display."

If she'd forgotten that Ajax was originally part of *this* crowd, his suggestion sent the message home clearly. The man did raise a good point, however. Even if they could find a place to survive until morning, everyone else was a sitting duck. She couldn't just leave them out here, despite the fact that it was their own doing. It wasn't right.

"Shit… we have to corral all these assholes, don't we?" Horace asked. It felt good to know she wasn't the only sane person left in the madhouse, and Cori nodded in agreement.

"I think so. Tabitha said Mr. Giggles doesn't like crowds. Maybe if we can get them all into one location, he'll keep his distance. Or, if he does show up, he has to fight the entire group at once. Unless he actually is magical, there's little chance he'd win that one."

Horace hesitated for a moment, truly considering his next words. "But if he *is* actually magical, wouldn't we be leading them all to a slaughter?"

The stares from Cori and Ajax were about what he'd expected, hence the initial hesitation. Still, he'd said it, so Horace opted to see things through. "I'm not saying I think he is, necessarily. Just pointing out that if we consider it even a possibility, we have to look at what the consequences would be. On the off chance that this asshole really is an immortal murderer, wouldn't we be penning in a ton of targets and forcing him to come work through them by getting rid of stragglers?"

It was a very good point, assuming one was willing to entertain the idea of magic. Before either could engage in debate on the subject, a new noise hit their ears. Static and crackling, the sounds of the large, bullhorn-like speakers that were situated through the park. They were controlled via the main operating center at the hotel, meaning at least these were connected to the generator, not unexpectedly coming to life like the roller coaster. Cori felt a wave of relief wash over her; all was not lost after all. They still had competent allies, and perhaps one of them was about to unveil a new plan.

"Good evening, everyone. My name is Jesse, and I'm your Safety Supervisor for this outing. No doubt by now you've heard about a few of the accidents we've found people experiencing. I'm here to reassure you that, despite the wild rumors flying around, there is certainly not a killer among us. Just people not paying attention and getting themselves hurt. We're requesting that everyone please return to the hotel as soon as possible. While we know many of you are engaged in various activities, we've set up another round of food to enjoy, as well as collected all the 'party supplies' you brought along from your bags. If you want to claim them, be at the hotel within the next half an hour."

For a full half-minute, none of them spoke, until Cori finally said the words they were all thinking. "Assuming Horace is right, just for the sake of argument, you could also corral everyone together if you wanted to see them all slaughtered."

"Or wanted to hunt the killer and needed bait for a trap." This came from Ajax, who met their surprised glances with a shrug. "A lot of us are ambitious. Saving everyone's lives from a madman would definitely be one way to earn some clout."

He had a point, there were multiple reasons someone could set up a situation like this. Nevertheless, Cori didn't trust that voice. There was a part of it that just felt off, in a way she couldn't put a finger on. There was no stopping the crowd, though. Already, they were shouting and scrambling, some darting off toward the hotel without even properly donning their pants.

Suddenly feeling very tired for reasons that had nothing to do with the late hour, Cori steeled herself and faced the others. "Sounds like we're going to need a plan of our own."

17

The business crowd was milling about at the hotel. A few stragglers remained, although with Ghoul doing a sweep in the nearby area, none would be alive to stray Mr. Giggles from his course. Knowing where he would go allowed them to be ready for his arrival, a standard tactic from their usual hunts. Normally, they would have readied drugs or traps, something to immobilize their prey and extend the killing process. Given that Mr. Giggles was inhumanly strong as well as unbothered by anything other than a direct strike from the axe; such tactics were unlikely to have any effect.

Facing such an advanced opponent, Jester had no choice but to take things back to basics. No needles or traps, no cunning electronic trickery, Jester's only resources were the bodies he could control. Earlier in the night, it would have given him three pawns to play with, but Wolf and Burlap had been lost in the collection of information. Even dead, they'd been useful. Wolf alerted them to a threat, and Burlap's demise helped Jester learn his prey's weakness. Were Jester capable of mourning, he would have done so. Instead, he decided that he would frame them as competent, when telling their exploits to the next batch.

This was already his fourth crew. None of the others ever quite had Jester's knack for survival. Sometimes they made mistakes on a job, sometimes they failed him. Either way, the fate was the same. If he could have only chosen one to keep from this lot, it would have been Burlap, but Ghoul was a nice runner-up. She might even survive what was coming, although Jester certainly wasn't counting on it.

A whiff of urine on the wind caught Jester's nose. Looking down the midway, he could see the floppy-eared figure heading in the direction of the hotel. They knew he would come through here, it was one of the few spots in the park where one had to cross in the open, no hidden tunnels connected this section to the hotel. One step at a time, keeping a surprisingly brisk pace, Mr. Giggles made his way forward. Thunder rumbled overhead, the dense clouds still refusing to rain. That might have cooled the night down; instead they had only the tension of waiting electricity crackling through the air.

Ghoul darted out from the side of a booth, racing past and slicing Mr. Giggles across the back. He spun around to swing for her, but she was already out of reach. She didn't vanish entirely, instead she stayed close, backing up steadily. Mr. Giggles gave chase, no consideration for even the possibility that she could be leading him into a trap. Jester understood why, now that he'd learned more of this man. They were dealing with an apex predator, something that ruled his domain. Why would he fear a trap? He was the thing that people were meant to fear.

Darting in and out, Ghoul managed a few cuts on Mr. Giggles, not that any of them bled or bothered him. The wounds didn't even linger, closing up after a few seconds. All that kept Ghoul alive was the fact that he was moving more slowly than on the carousel, slightly favoring his injury. The axe attacks, at least, left lasting damage. That was why they'd built a plan around the tool, rudimentary as it was. Draw him out, grab his attention, lead him right where they wanted. As usual, Ghoul was doing excellent work. They were nearly in range.

Finally, Ghoul took Mr. Giggles around another turn. They were in the center of the section, a kiddie area filled with dead-eyed stares of lifeless displays and decorations. Next to Ghoul, a statue of Dr. Puddin had a plastic sign advocating for kids to only smoke menthol cigarettes, the doctor's choice. Apparently they had been some cross-promotion with the real Mr. Giggles' new career in the later years. As their Mr. Giggles grasped for Ghoul, who was panting audibly from her efforts, Jester stepped out silently from behind the statue of Dr. Puddin.

With time to aim, it was a trivial matter. One chop to the neck, and this would be done. Jester reared back, lining up his shot, and prepared to end this. It had been an interesting evening, but once again, he was the victor.

"Don't!"

The voice came right as Jester swung, causing Mr. Giggles to jerk around suddenly. It wasn't enough to make Jester miss; however, it did turn his decapitation swing into a blow on Mr. Giggles' chest. The axe bit deep, gouging into Mr. Giggles' pectoral muscles before coming to a halt.

His scream was near-deafening, and not even the most salient problem of the moment. From his body, crackling energy exploded in all directions, washing over the area like a wave. Suddenly, lights flickered on, slow-moving electronics kicked into motion, and the noise of dozens of kid-distracting devices all shrieked to life.

Jester felt a hand on his shoulder, dragging him away as the rogue current left him momentarily stunned and twitching. Looking up, he found himself staring into the face of the woman who had been running the minivan shuttle. He remembered her, just as he remembered every drone on the property in case they had been useful to exploit. Why she was here currently, now that he had no information on. Fortunately, she was the chatty sort.

"If you cut off his head, he just keeps on going and you're down a target. You need to hit the heart, and bury the axe in it. Bad news is that he throws off those shock waves when he's seriously hurt. Good news is that it takes him about ten minutes to recharge. Thanks for your help, though I'm not sure what the masks are about, I appreciate the aid."

She rose to her feet, a surprisingly steely expression in her eyes. "Although I do wish you'd held onto the axe."

For the first time, Jester realized his hands were empty. After the attack and the blast, he'd never yanked it out of Mr. Giggles' chest, and the opportunity was sadly past. Even from the ground, he could easily see Mr. Giggles jerk the weapon free, clutching it in his hands. New sparks were running between the killer and the axe, a duo reunited at last.

While she'd left herself exposed, Jester made no attempt to cut the woman down. He felt nothing as mundane as gratitude, but with the situation shifting so rapidly, it wouldn't hurt to let her go first. They might get useful information out of watching, and if she succeeded, then they would have a far more human target to play with.

The videographers had chosen the wrong location to lie in wait. They'd wrongfully assumed Mr. Giggles would take the least watched route, rather than the most direct one, and so were a few sections over when the fight began. As soon as they heard Tabby's yell of warning, they started in that direction, giving them an excellent view of the electrical explosion that brought the kiddie section to life.

A swinging wing from a sign promoting Albatross Esquire's Legally Delicious Ice Cream nearly clipped Horace in the skull as it sprang into motion, not missing a beat. Looking around, Cori could scarcely believe her eyes. Electricity alone didn't explain all this; these items had been left neglected and exposed to the elements for years. Even with power, they shouldn't be running, and certainly not so seamlessly. There really did seem to be no way around it: there was magic afoot tonight.

If the mechanisms suddenly working weren't enough proof, they rounded a corner just in time to see Mr. Giggles, looking as horrible as described, pulling an axe from his pecs like it was no more than a thorn. The dead eyes of the rabbit mask turned to and fro, before looking down at the slender fellow in a jester mask.

Cori wanted to wonder who the fuck that guy was, but she had more dire concerns at the moment. Namely the supposedly immortal killer who, according to Tabby, had just reclaimed the only thing that could stop him. Behind Mr. Giggles, Cori caught sight of another figure wearing some sort of ugly mask. They had the advantage of numbers, it nothing else.

"Nuh uh, you ugly bastard. No starting the new course until you finish your last meal. Come on, you dead mother fucker. Come try and kill me like you killed my friends." Tabby whipped off her hat, exposing a long plume of dark hair tinged by streaks of gray. She wasn't that old, and given the context clues, Cori was guessing that coloration came from the stress of knowing there was an immortal magic killer in the world. "You know me. You want me. I'm the one who put you away last time. You never stop chasing when you pick a target. Well, you haven't caught me yet, have you?"

Whether Mr. Giggles was cognizant of everything around him was hard to say with only a charred mask to look at, but his head definitely moved from the man in the jester mask to Tabby at the sound of her voice. A step forward, heavy and sure, definitely in Tabby's direction, was all the warning before Mr. Giggles charged. The swings of the axe were wild, but even from a distance everyone could feel the power coming off of them. If even one connected, that would be the end of whoever it hit. Thankfully, Tabby didn't get caught by any of the first swipes; she was already darting around, back in the direction Mr. Giggles had come from.

"Everyone, be ready. He's going to throw down the axe after a few more failed attempts. That tool is for cutting down generic fodder, the tough ones, he likes to finish by hand."

"But he just got it back, and you told him what you're planning," Cori pointed out, well aware that she too was in earshot.

"Doesn't matter. There's no thought in there. Just patterns and a drive to kill." Tabby ducked another swing, although not by much. Sweat was running down her face already, the effort obviously harder than it had been decades prior. "And make sure it's a girl who grabs it. I don't know why, but in the end, it's always a woman who puts him down."

Horace choked somewhere in his throat. "All of this, and the idea that the 'final girl' trope is based in reality is what seems the most insane."

Since the woman with the ugly mask was behind Tabby, and therefore penned in by Mr. Giggles, that left the task to Cori. She barely had time to realize that before Tabby's words came true. With a mighty blow, Mr. Giggles embedded his axe in the statue of Dr. Puddin, creating a line across the diagonal of her face. Tabby stepped back further, pulling Mr. Giggles away from his axe as he gave chase. With two hands grabbing, dodging became far more difficult, and Tabby was slower as consequence.

Not wasting time, Cori darted forward, gripping the shaft of the axe. Sparks flew along her fingers at its touch, an interesting detail that she immediately ignored. Pulling hard, she found the axe hard to budge. Chancing a look over, Cori noticed that Tabby was barely staying out of reach. Soon, her luck or stamina would fail. Putting all she had into one mighty tug, Cori managed to yank the axe free. A yelp from Tabby signaled that time was nearly up.

Even in these circumstances, Cori wasn't someone who went for the kill on instinct. Seeing Mr. Giggles grabbing Tabby by the throat, however, did spur her to action. With a well-aimed swing, she chopped off the right arm gripping Tabby at the elbow. It dropped, hanging from Tabby's neck where the grip had loosened without giving up entirely. Before she could think, Cori took another swing at Mr. Giggles' right leg. She only caught it below the knee, yet the blade slid easily through, sending him tumbling to the ground. No blood, only inhuman noises of pain coming from within the mask.

Down a leg and an arm, Mr. Giggles had lost most of his mobility, although he did continue to crawl along the ground. Nearby, Tabby managed to pry off the hand clutching at her, tossing it away from Mr. Giggles. "Thanks. Was running out of time there." She rubbed her neck a few times, then held out her hand. "If you like, I can handle the rest for you. We can put this night to an end."

The blade was swift and sure, singing along Tabby's bruised throat and opening up a hot spray of blood. As she fell, Tabby's corpse revealed the woman in a hideous mask holding a blood-covered knife.

"Useful as you were, this night ends when we say so, and not a moment before."

Cori stood there, frozen, unable to process what had just occurred. They'd done it. They'd won. Mr. Giggles was on the ground, still dragging himself around but otherwise helpless. All that was left was finishing the job. It was supposed to be over; they were supposed to be safe. These people weren't magical killers brought forth by unspecified and slightly ludicrous supernatural forces. Tabby's killer was panting, with a small trail of blood along one shoulder where she'd taken a cut from the axe. This woman was human, which made her action all the more unforgivable.

"Why… why did you kill her?"

"Because she was unguarded, and it was fun." As the woman stepped better into the light coming off the various displays, Cori could see how twisted that mask really was. Rotting, horrendous flesh formed from plastic. It was hard to even look at, yet Cori dared not turn away. "Now, if you hand over that axe, I think Jester might be willing to spare one of your cohorts."

Quickly, damn quickly, Cori looked over to Horace and

Ajax. The man in the clown mask, Jester, had moved behind them both. She couldn't see what he was doing, but the distressed expressions on her co-workers' faces painted a clear picture, and not a pretty one at that. His voice was controlled and smooth in spite of the circumstances. "Ghoul, take the axe and finish off the problem. After that, we can proceed with the evening."

In response, the woman, who evidently went by a fitting moniker, held out her hand and wiggled her fingers. "Hand it over. I can also take it the fun way, although your friends won't live long enough to watch the full show."

Any ideas of taking a swing vanished. Ghoul was right; they had Cori over a barrel. Even knowing it would probably cost them all their lives, she couldn't think of a better move than handing the axe over. Better to live for another few minutes and see if the situation changed. At worst, she would buy everyone a bit more time breathing. At best, maybe they'd manage to see another sunrise after all.

Taking a step back to get clear of Mr. Giggles' grasping hand, Cori held out the axe to Ghoul handle first. The murderer accepted the new weapon, a few sparks dancing along her fingers as they closed on the wooden shaft. Ghoul looked to Jester, who responded in the same even tone.

"In case that woman was right about the gender mattering, best you finish things off. Consider it a reward for your hard work this evening."

Ghoul's grip on the axe tightened, and Cori thought she saw something like a smile twitching under that horrific mask. "It will be an honor." She moved toward Mr. Giggles, lining up her first shot carefully. Just as she was lifting the weapon, a thought appeared to strike her, as Ghoul looked back to Cori over her shoulder.

"If you want to try and sneak attack me, feel free. I do love the thrill of a good surpri—" Ghoul's words were cut off as a hand suddenly closed around her ankle. While she'd been taunting Cori, Mr. Giggles had gotten a good grip on the ground and hurled himself forward, eliminating the distance between him and his weapon.

There was an audible crunch as he destroyed Ghoul's ankle. She screamed, swinging the axe as she fell. It managed to land once, carving into Mr. Giggles' right shoulder. Since there was no arm there for him to use anyway, the effect was negligible. As Ghoul landed, Mr. Giggles grabbed for his weapon, forcing her to jerk it aside. An unexpected knee to the sternum weakened her grip, turning her maneuver into a rough toss, sending the axe clattering to the ground at Cori's feet.

Without waiting for permission, Cori snatched the axe back up. For a moment, she considered attacking Ghoul, but since Jester still had the other two in his clutches, that was too dangerous. If anything, he'd probably force her to give Ghoul the axe back. Maybe she should have left it on the ground after all.

"Give me that axe!" Ghoul demanded, trying to fight off Mr. Giggles despite her own newly crippled leg slowing her down. "Now!"

"Don't move." Despite the fact that Ghoul was screaming and Jester's voice refused to raise, Cori immediately knew which one to listen to. He was the one in charge, and if his demand happened to see Tabby's murderer killed, Cori had no objections.

"What?" Ghoul whipped her head over to Jester, a mistake as it turned out when Mr. Giggles managed to get his remaining hand wrapped around her shoulder. "Why?"

Jester shook his head. "You had the tools and the opportunity. If you've squandered them, then this is the fate you deserve. I won't deny a fellow predator his rightly earned kill."

"You... you're joking. Have her give me that damn axe. Help me!" Ghoul's voice was turning to a shriek as Mr. Giggles' grip tightened on her collarbone, easily hauling her further into his grip. The hand moved, clamping down on her neck, ignoring her struggles.

"Help yourself, or die and be quiet." No anger, no judgement, no mercy. No change at all. Nothing of this was affecting Jester in the slightest.

Perhaps Ghoul would have objected more, were she permitted more time; however, a sudden application of pressure from Mr. Giggles put an end to both her screams and the trail of blood left in her wake. Satisfied with his work, Mr. Giggles resumed his crawling, once more headed for Cori.

"That just leaves you, the final of our final girls," Jester noted. "Perhaps that driver was more right than she knew. Two attempts, both dead. Maybe it really does have to be the last of the ladies. How about you test the theory?"

Cori could already see how it would play out. She would either die at Mr. Giggles' hand, or succeed in stopping him only to be cut down by Jester seconds later. He'd just allowed his own partner to be killed; that didn't seem like the kind of man who was going to let them walk away from this. Right now, she had a weapon and a monster. Maybe she could do something with that.

"No."

By the time Cori looked back over, both Horace and Ajax were on the ground, blood pouring out from their backs. Zero hesitation, the moment she'd tried to rebel he'd cut both down. Her stomach twisted and her heart ached; she hadn't expected such swift reprisal. Giving in now wouldn't help them, though. She had to stop this. All of this. It had already cost plenty of lives, if hers was the last to pay to end things, then it would be a soul well-spent.

Mr. Giggles was a violent, thoughtless murderer. And oddly, that made him the better of the two men before Cori. At least he was cursed, trapped in this life. Jester had no such excuses. He wasn't magical or being re-animated. He was just a piece of shit who liked to hurt people. Moving largely on instinct, Cori hurriedly stepped over, putting Mr. Giggles between herself and Jester. She kept enough distance not to echo Ghoul's mistake, but otherwise stayed as near as she dared.

"You should have only killed one of them when I refused. Now you're out of threats to make." The axe was warm and heavy in her hands, like it wanted her to remember it was there, waiting to be used.

"Oh, I think I can still come up with a couple of new threats." A flash of metal appeared briefly in Jester's hands, yet he didn't actually come forward. Mr. Giggles had wiped out the rest of his crew, underestimating the blood-monger would only lead to his own undoing.

From around them, the sound of voices could be heard. Between the screaming and the sudden lightshow, they'd managed to attract the curiosity of the hotel guests. It was a stalemate, one that couldn't last for very long. Cori was torn. The arrival of the others could mean salvation, or it could provide Jester with more people to threaten.

"I wonder, if maybe there *is* some magic available to the women who last to the end. Because as much as I would love to cut you down, I am tempted to let you live. With the crowd closing in, my escape becomes more dangerous. Getting around a worthy foe to slice you up represents an unnecessary waste of time. Instead, allow me to make a simple offer. Give me the axe, and I will take my leave." Jester extended his arm, hand open. "With my team dead, it would be time to retreat regardless. Obviously I'll be bringing the magic weapon along as well. Whether I leave another corpse to be found in the process is entirely up to you."

An immediate denial died on Cori's tongue as Mr. Giggles flopped closer, forcing her to reposition. Even chopped up, he couldn't do anything but try to kill. The man was trapped in an endless cycle just as much as his victims. Cursed. Sparks flew along the axe's handle as she adjusted her grip. Cursed, and connected to this axe. Tabby said it always went the same. Mr. Giggles would rise, kill, be slain by the axe, and rise again when it was disturbed. He couldn't leave the park, supposedly, but what if someone tried to take away his weapon? True, it might mean losing the only way to stop this monster; however, the old ways weren't solving the problem. Maybe it was time to try something new.

"All yours." Cori tossed the axe over Mr. Giggles, where it landed loudly at Jester's feet.

In a flash, he'd scooped it up, eyeing Cori and Mr. Giggles as he did. Whether or not Tabby was right about it needing to be a final girl had yet to be confirmed, and if he pressed his luck it could go either way. They were dealing with magic, meaning logic and reason were useless tools in assessing the outcomes. Ultimately, Jester's best bet for survival was to do as he'd promised. With a casual wave, he ran, vanishing into the shadows after mere seconds.

Cori waited as long as she dared before scuttling around Mr. Giggles and running over to her friends. Both had a substantial amount of blood pooled around them, but as Cori took hold of Horace's neck to check for a pulse, she heard a ragged wheeze of a breath squeeze out.

"This… fucking… sucks."

"You're alive?" Cori almost jumped back in shock. Checking the wound, she found that whatever weapon Jester used had the misfortune of being knocked slightly aside by a spare battery pack tucked into Horace's waistband. The blade had still done serious damage, but the shift in angle might have spared Horace's organs.

"Been better." His words were coming faster now that he was drawing breath.

With hope in her heart, Cori checked Ajax, only to find that he hadn't been so lucky. Thunder boomed as more lightning tore through the sky overhead, so common that it had slowly become background noise through the night. As best she could, Cori covered Ajax's face. It would have to do until they could get proper authorities here.

"Don't worry," Cori told him. "We shouldn't move you, but once the others find us there's bound to be someone with first aid."

Carefully, wary eyes still on Mr. Giggles' struggling form, she moved back in front of Horace. "Until then, I'll keep an eye on *him*."

———

Escape was simple. Although he hadn't informed the team, Jester brought more parachutes than they would need for the job, squirreling some away throughout the park during the day. It was best to have an emergency exit strategy, one he could use on his own if needed. In his race from the midway, it was a simple matter to grab one of his hidden parachutes and fasten it on before proceeding to the cliff.

Giggletime Mountain's steep drop was protected by three security fences intended to keep kids and drunks from accidentally wandering off the side. Those safety measures had been undermined by weather and Father Time, however, so breaking the locks in anticipation for this evening had been a trivial matter. With the route already cleared, Jester tore through the gates in seconds, arriving at the steep cliff edge. It looked out on a large wooded area with a few roads cutting through.

From here, he would need to aim for the landing zone where a car was stashed and waiting. After that, all he had to do was shed the mask and Jester became just another traveler exploring the wonders of nature. The outing certainly hadn't gone as planned, and losing his team was an unexpected wrinkle, but it wasn't as if he'd come away empty-handed. Jester now knew that magic was real, which opened up enough possibilities on its own, and he'd even snagged an actual enchanted weapon. What it could do, how he could use it, there were countless ideas Jester couldn't wait to explore.

Despite the brisk winds, Jester felt secure as he leapt into the air. He popped his chute as soon as he was far enough from the cliff, catching the wind and sailing away from Giggletime Mountain. Overhead, the thunder roared even louder than before. Jester took a moment to appreciate the vast power of the storm. He respected all great displays of power, be they of men or gods.

A new noise reached his eyes, like static from a television set. Looking down, he noticed the axe crackling with electricity, far more than it had shown so far. At the next clap of thunder, it brightened, as if in response. Jester didn't know where this was going, only that it appeared bad. He struggled, trying to get a hand around the axe he'd so carefully attached to his hip, but the winds demanded he keep control of his parachute.

Glancing around, he could see the huge bolts of lightning dancing in the sky overhead. Jester never heard the last clap of thunder, because fast as it was, the lightning was always a little faster. When the light cleared, there was nothing more than a burning section of canvas sheet, the last remains of the parachute, drifting through the sky.

The first drop of rain caught Cori in the forehead. In seconds, they were surrounded by what felt like an earnest attempt at a flood. After a whole night of build-up, the rain had finally come, dousing the entire park. One by one, the displays went dark around them once more. Lights flickered off, movement turned back to stillness, and the eerie old music faded away. And Mr. Giggles had the strangest reaction of all.

As the rain struck, he stopped struggling. Streams of water ran down his body, turning dark the moment it hit as the drops washed decades of grime from his body. No, it was doing more than that, Cori realized. The rain was washing all of Mr. Giggles away. He was smearing, like a painting tossed in a tub, vanishing into those dark streams. A section of the mask's bottom fell away, revealing the lower half of a face. The mouth turned upward, briefly forming a smile before mouthing two simple words.

"Thank you."

The rain surged suddenly, making it impossible to see even the few feet between them. When the surge died down, returning back to a normal torrent, Mr. Giggles was nowhere to be seen. Only a dark stain remained on the ground where he had been.

EPILOGUE

For as bad as the corporate raiders and insurance evaluators were at anything involving real danger, they turned out to be savants of covering shit up. After the storm, when morning broke, a delivery of more food and liquor that had been placed the night before showed up to find the broken bridge. From there, it was a short while until the proper people were notified. Once phone service was restored, a lot of the folks still smeared in drugs, grime, and other… fluids, all began shouting into receivers about "do you know who I am this" and "I can have your job for that." They were assholes, but they got results.

Before noon, emergency services were flown in. Horace, thanks to some quickly applied first aid, survived to be helicoptered out. In exchange for some hastily prepared non-disclosures, Horace's medical bills were put under the company's name for them to handle. She and Horace would also be getting a substantial pay-out in return for their silence about what they'd seen the executives doing. Any other day and Cori would have chased the story, but between a night with killers and Horace's wounds, she decided that focusing her film on the legend of a supernatural murderer had more appeal anyway. Cutting around the few shots of misbehaving executives was worth it to see her friend taken care of.

Especially since she was down a crew member. That one hadn't really hit yet, even after someone found Bernard's corpse and called her down to confirm it. Cori's hands had felt numb as she stripped the recording gear from his body. The whole time, her mind was screaming at her that this was wrong, and callous. She knew better. Bernard loved the craft more than he liked most people. He'd want his final footage used, all the more so if it cost him his life. Cori hadn't figured out how she would break the news to Horace yet, that was a concern for once he was stable.

An emergency bridge was set-up over the destroyed section, permitting everyone to walk across the gap and step into one of the waiting limo buses that was waiting to bring them all back into town. Cori filed in along with the others, taking a seat near the window. As the bus began to move, driving back toward civilization, her eyes lingered on the amusement park. Perhaps now that it was finally over, someone would rebuild this place, turn it back into the destination of joy it was intended as.

Her video might even help, eventually. Scary as it was bound to be, Giggletime Mountain could potentially see a resurgence once people knew it was safe to return.

Several hours later, the sun fell below the horizon once more. As it did, a single cloud formed overhead. No massive storm, no torrent of thunder. One cloud, that released one bolt of lightning into the center of the park, leaving a dark stain on the concrete ground.

From that stain, dust and darkness rose, taking a new form. This was not a lumbering behemoth in a bunny-rabbit's head, however. It was lean, quick, with an axe clutched in his hands. His face was hidden behind a smooth ceramic mask with simple marking. Overhead, the faded remains of a banner were covered in the same swirling dust, clearing seconds later to reveal a new banner that could have been hung that very morning.

"Mr. Smiley welcomes you all to the new and improved Giggletime Mountain."

THE END

ABOUT THE AUTHOR

Drew Hayes is an author from Texas who has now found time and gumption to publish a few books. He graduated from Texas Tech with a B.A. in English, because evidently he's not familiar with what the term "employable" means. Drew has been called one of the most profound, prolific, and talented authors of his generation, but a table full of drunks will say almost anything when offered a round of free shots. Drew feels kind of like a D-bag writing about himself in the third person like this. He does appreciate that you're still reading, though.

Drew would like to sit down and have a beer with you. Or a cocktail. He's not here to judge your preferences. Drew is terrible at being serious, and has no real idea what a snippet biography is meant to convey anyway. Drew thinks you are awesome just the way you are. That part, he meant. You can reach Drew with questions or movie offers at Novelist-Drew@gmail.com Drew is off to go high-five random people, because who doesn't love a good high-five? No one, that's who.

Read or purchase more of his work at his site: Drew-HayesNovels.com